THE LIVING AND THE REST

JOSÉ EDUARDO AGUALUSA

THE LIVING AND
THE REST

Translated from the Portuguese by
Daniel Hahn

MACLEHOSE PRESS
QUERCUS · LONDON

First published in the Portuguese language as *Os vivos e os outros* by
Quetzal Editores, Lisbon, in 2020
First published in Great Britain in 2023 by

MacLehose Press
an imprint of Quercus
Carmelite House
50 Victoria Embankment
London EC4Y 0DZ

Funded by the DGLAB/Culture and the Camões, IP – Portugal

The following extracts have been translated from the Portuguese by Daniel Hahn: lines
from Ana Mafalda Leite, "A lenda da criação" in *Outras Fronteiras* (Maputo: Cavalo do
Mar, 2019); lines from Job Sipitali, *Raízes Cantam* (Lisbon: Perfil Criativo, 2017);
lines from Ruy Duarte de Carvalho, "Sinal" in *Lavra: poesia reunida 1970–2000*
(Lisbon: Cotovia, 2005)

A CIP catalogue record for this book is available from the British Library.

ISBN (PB) 978 1 52942 175 0
ISBN (eBook) 978 1 52942 176 7

10 9 8 7 6 5

Designed and typeset in Haarlemmer by Libanus Press Ltd
Printed and bound in Great Britain by Clays Ltd, Elcograf S.p.A.

Papers used by MacLehose Press are from well-managed forests and
other responsible sources.

For Yara, who gave me the Island of Mozambique

THE FIRST DAY

In the beginning there was chauta *(god) and the motionless earth*
one day a huge lightning-flash drew in the skies
the rain
which brought man to the earth and all the animals.

ANA MAFALDA LEITE, "The Creation Story"

I

The sea still hangs from the living-room window, like a slightly crooked picture, but it's no longer the same sea that Daniel Benchimol found when he first arrived on the island, three years ago. He has swum in it countless times. He's familiar with its currents and tides. He knows where the wrecked ships lie, and the galleons, the dhows and the pangayas. He has visited the beaches and the islands. He has looked the whales in the eye and watched them leave.

After we have come to know them intimately, places become different. The writer pulls his chair over to the window and sits facing the light, drinking iced tea. Moira is still asleep, holding her swollen belly with both hands. She too is no longer the same woman he first met, on a splendid April afternoon, on the broad veranda of a colonial mansion in Cape Town.

Intimacy is paradise – and hell. We fall in love with something we do not yet know. Love is what happens to passion once intimacy settles in. With any luck. And he, Daniel, has been lucky. With Moira and with her island.

He puts on a pair of trainers and goes out into the salty morning air. He runs down Rua dos Combatentes, by the railings, and then along the beach, as far as the Santo António church, pursued by some kids shouting encouragement – "Keep going, tio Daniel!", "Faster, tio!" He doubles back and returns home. Moira is waiting in the kitchen, with the table already set. She holds a glass out to him.

"Juice from our lemons. Drink it!"

Daniel does just that. Then he takes a quick shower and joins her, at the table.

"Have they all arrived, our writers?" he asks, as he breaks open a mucate, one of those local bread rolls made with rice flour and coconut milk, and spreads it with peanut butter. "They're going to cause us a lot of trouble."

"It'll be fun," replies Moira. "And no, they haven't all arrived yet. We've got a good team. It's going to go well."

She is wearing a wide boubou, which can't disguise her nine-month belly. She has hidden her thick dreads inside a tall red and yellow turban, which seems to lengthen her face.

"And the baby? How's she doing?"

"Or he! Sleeping just now."

"It's a girl. I'm sure of it. She's going to be called Tetembua."

"Boy or girl, you've got to say goodbye now – I need to head off to work."

Daniel kisses her bellybutton and then her lips. Moira leaves. He goes into the study and sits down at the computer. He writes for half an hour. His telephone announces the arrival of a new message. It's from Uli Lima Levy:

"What are your plans for this morning?"

"I was waiting for you to wake up," the Angolan replies. "I'll come and meet you."

Uli had arrived on the island the previous day. He was tired, after a long tour through Spain, France and Germany. They'd had dinner together at Karibu, a restaurant serving honest food, as Moira put it. Dishonest food, to her, was any industrial cooking, which used vegetables treated with pesticides, battery chickens and fish bred in farms. They'd eaten tuna in ginger sauce, and then Daniel had accompanied his friend to the hotel, the Villa Sands, which was housing two other writers, both of them Angolan: Ofélia Eastermann and Luzia Valente.

2

Ofélia Eastermann wakes up with four lines dancing around in her head:

"*On Friday midnights, Ofélia took the sky, | and wove it with infinity. | Meanwhile, the breeze flowed between palm fronds, | like the spirits' river-sounds.*"

She gets up and jots them down in a small red-covered notebook, on which she has written in coarse black letters: "Dream trash".

Whenever somebody asks her politely "Where are you from?", Ofélia shuts her eyes and sees the rough stone beds of the watercourses down which, in the rainy season, sudden rivers flow. She sees the slow gravel paths between the brambles, the rusty carcasses of the ships, the wild dogs hovering over the dunes. She sees a woman with skin dyed ochre-red, thick braids, with a little boy in her arms. "I'm from the South," she answers. On other occasions, hoping to shock her interlocutors, which she does often, she chooses a different formulation: "I am from all the beds where I've been happy."

On one occasion, during an interview, she got irritated by one of the interviewer's questions ("You were born in the south of Angola, you were brought up in Lisbon and live in Rio de Janeiro. So really, do you feel more Angolan, Portuguese or Brazilian?"), and, since indignation is a kind of intoxication, she lost her cool, frightening the journalist with a shout that now appears on hundreds of literary sites, good and bad and terrible ones: "I come from the palm trees – fuck it! Not Angolan, or Brazilian, or Portuguese! Wherever there's a palm tree, that's where I'm from! I'm from the sea and the forests and the savannas. I come from a world that hasn't arrived yet: with no god, no kings, no borders and no armies."

Ofélia hates the line, but can do nothing to stop it spreading. People who have never read her poetry, and never will, share that lyrical outburst, like conspirators exchanging watchwords and passwords. Her Brazilian publisher commissioned a T-shirt with the words "I come from the palm trees – fuck it!" to put on sale in bookshops and at literary festivals. Ofélia earns more from the T-shirts than from her books. She gets up, thinking about all this, and looks out the window. She sees Daniel arriving, hurriedly – he's always nineteen to the dozen, as if he has a permanent gale at his back, pushing him on. Uli Lima is waiting for him on a chair by the pool. Unlike the Angolan, Uli radiates a natural calm, he lives in perpetual Sunday. The two friends exchange a hug, and when she sees them, the poet thinks she'd like to have a writer friend. Male or female. Though a woman seems even more unlikely, she's always got along better with men. She misses having someone with whom to swap books and opinions, to show crooked lines of verse. She knows what people say about her: she's arrogant, envious, vain and crazy. Crazy's fine. Crazy doesn't offend her. Being crazy means rebelling against the norm, and the norm is corruption, flattery, obsequiousness. As for vanity, she's perfectly well aware of what she's worth, and sees no reason to hide it, modesty is a virtue for the mediocre. I'm also not arrogant, she thinks, what I am is direct. Many people confuse boldness with arrogance. Envious, oh yes, that's true, she can't help that. She does get irritated at the success of morons. Daniel, for example, was a decent journalist, she remembers reading one of his reports, really interesting, about a village that disappeared during the civil war. Since people liked reading his reports and gave him lots of little pats on the back – "Hey, nice one, you write really well!" – the good fellow convinced himself he could be a writer and published three novels that were naïve, almost childish, yet also unbearably pretentious. They sold very well. This hadn't surprised her. People appreciate simple-minded little stories disguised as complex fables: talking giraffes, ludicrous mysteries, ready-made life lessons straight off the shelf. Uli annoys her even more because, well, he really *does* have a tremendous talent, a sense of rhythm, a prodigious facility for creating plots. The guy writes effortlessly. He triumphs without breaking a sweat. He's like those cowboys from the old westerns, who'd confront fifteen bandits in a saloon, punching and kicking, and finish the fight with his hat still on his head and not so much as a crease in his immaculately white shirt. Somebody really should have wrung his neck at birth. On top of all that, he is a handsome man, charming, with a deep, slightly hoarse voice, which can turn even the cold heart of the rocks into throbbing flesh. Yes, she envies him – but she'd sleep with him most willingly.

She looks at herself in the mirror. She's gained fifteen kilos in recent years, and she's lost her waist. On the other hand, her breasts have filled out. She has thick, dishevelled hair, which makes her look fierce, and wide eyes that shine like mirrors. Her eyes have not grown old. She still uses them successfully to attract the unwary. She smiles at herself. Then she chooses a light dress, in pitanga-red, she paints her lips the identical colour and goes down to the bar, beside the swimming pool, in search of a coffee to bring her back to life.

3

The Hotel Villa Sands art gallery occupies a rectangular building, painted white, opposite the fish market. The entrance opens into a spacious atrium, very well lit, in which canvases and photographs are displayed, and this hall gives access in turn to a small inner garden. This is where the bar is located. Cornelia Oluokun, seated at one of the tables, is drinking a coffee while using her phone to exchange messages with her husband. Standing opposite the Nigerian writer, looking at her in bemusement, is a girl. The child has followed Cornelia from the hotel where she's staying, the Terraço das Quitandas. Her very white hair, tall and curly, floats like a soft cloud above her head. If somebody were to enter at this moment and see them like this, one opposite the other, the Nigerian woman in a large boubou in various shades of blue, the girl in a little white dress, they could easily mistake the whole thing for an art installation. "The goddess and her angel", that could be one possible title.

"I don't know why I've come," writes Cornelia. "The plane hadn't even landed and I was already regretting it."

"You always say that," Pierre messages back. "Your presence is important. We're always complaining there aren't many literary festivals in Africa. We've got to support the ones that do crop up. Besides, I've been looking at photos of the Ilha de Moçambique. Colonial mansions, wonderful beaches. History and nature all together in one space. Reminds me of Zanzibar. I should have gone with you."

"No. I should have stayed with you, writing."

"You said you were going because the journey would take you out of your comfort zone and that might get you writing again – remember?"

"Terrible idea. I want to get out of here."

"But why?"

"Half this city's in ruins. The other half is a slum."

"So?"

"There's an albino girl following me everywhere, like a puppy."

"Really?"

Cornelia takes a photo of the girl and sends it over.

"You thought I was hallucinating?"

"She's so pretty! I still think she's a hallucination."

"Hallucinations don't let you take their picture."

"Most don't. But you've always had some really solid hallucinations. I think this one's marvellous. Aren't you in a café? Buy her a croissant."

"You think they make croissants in this dump?"

"A toasted sandwich, then. Something. What's her name?"

"How the hell should I know?"

"Ask her."

"I don't speak Portuguese."

"Ask in English. Even if she doesn't speak the language, she'll understand."

Cornelia puts down her phone and looks at the girl.

"What's your name?"

The girl shakes her head, making her magnificent crown of clouds tremble.

"Ainur," she murmurs.

Cornelia picks up her phone again. She writes:

"Her name's Ainur."

"Now order something for her to eat."

The girl turns around and runs out.

"She's run away," writes Cornelia. "Kids are scared of me."

"She doesn't look frightened in the photo. She looks fascinated. I had that exact same expression when I first saw you myself."

"You didn't run away when I asked your name."

"I was amazed. I was terrified. I really did want to run away, but it was impossible. If I remember correctly, there were eight hundred people in front of us – and they were all there for you."

"Ha ha! Leave it to you to make me laugh."

"It's my profession, and my destiny. I live to make you smile. Don't forget I'm your official enlightener."

Cornelia Oluokun's face breaks into a genuine smile. She gestures to the waitress, a thin, shy girl, who walks over slowly. She asks for another coffee and a croissant. Yes, they do sell croissants there. And they're not at all bad.

4

More than the old Indo-Portuguese furniture, brought over centuries earlier from Goa, what really enchants Jude D'Souza is the light. The air that supports it seems much older than the venerable armchairs, the tête-à-têtes, the tables and writing desks that fill the spacious halls of the old Palace of the Captains-General. The soft splendour that gilds the floorboards and sweetens the angles of the furniture must have been stored there ever since they built the place, in 1610, as a school for the Society of Jesus. He makes a note of the date on his phone, while he listens to the guide, a curious lad, who speaks decent English and shows an interest in what a Nigerian man – the first he's met – has come to do on the island.

Jude asks if he can take a photo of him standing next to one of the windows, looking out to sea, the features of his beautiful Arab face in that ancient glow. The young man laughs (his name is Juma) and strikes a pose, pulling in his stomach and puffing out his chest. The writer takes the Leica out of his rucksack and clicks three times. "OK!" he says, and when Juma relaxes, he clicks again. Then he takes a photo of a writing desk. He sends the two photos to his iPhone, and uploads them to Instagram. "Juma, guide at the Ilha de Moçambique Museum, showing me the light from a dead time" is the caption of the first photo. Under the second, he writes: "If I had a desk like this, I'm sure I'd write more. I'm sure I'd write better." When he leaves the Ilha de Moçambique Museum, an hour later, he can't resist opening Instagram. Each of the photos already has more than three thousand likes and hundreds of comments.

5

"I'm going in," Luzia announces, taking off her skirt and blouse. She removes her sandals and sits, in her bikini, with her feet in the calm darkness of the water. Ofélia releases the straps of her dress and stands up, letting it slip down to her feet. She isn't wearing a bra. She kneels down on the deck, next to the young woman.

"Well, girl, are we doing this or what?"

"I'm just summoning up the courage."

"You're welcome to go in, as far as I'm concerned," says Daniel. "But if a bolt of lightning hits the water, it's very likely you'll die of electrocution."

"Daniel's right about that," Uli agrees. "I didn't think you'd be wanting to swim when I arranged the thunderstorm."

Luzia takes her feet out of the water. She gets up.

"You people are annoying," she says, pretending to be irritated.

Ofélia does go in. She swims towards the storm.

Abdul has worked at the bar at the Hotel Villa Sands for five years. He's already seen many women stripping off on the deck, next to the pool. Some of them are only topless. Others take off all their clothes and stretch out on the loungers, their skin damp and very white, like panna cotta. Jan had warned him: "If any woman takes her clothes off, don't just stand there, like an owl, with your eyes glued to her body. Pretend nothing's happening. In Europe we like taking our clothes off, and not just in the saunas, but also on beaches, and in parks, whenever we get a bit of sun." Abdul would make a huge effort not to look at the European women's dazzling asses. As he'd explained to his grandmother, Dona Cinema, that morning while they were breakfasting, his job was not an easy one.

The darkness opens up suddenly into a quiet radiance.

Uli smiles at Luzia.

"I know I shouldn't boast, but this really is a very beautiful night."

The sea is still smooth. The biggest swimming pool in the world, that's what Luzia called it. And then another lightning-flash, and another and another, without the rumble of the thunder ever reaching them.

"You've clearly put a lot of work into it," Daniel smiles.

Then he falls silent. They all do, the three of them, as their eyes follow Ofélia's silhouette, cut out against the black gleam of the water, as she returns towards them now with elegant strokes.

"That woman is brave!" remarks Daniel.

Luzia looks at him angrily.

"Because she's swimming with lightning or because she's too old to be showing her breasts?"

"She's not old," Daniel defends himself. "You've got to be really young to swim with the lightning."

"And to show your breasts," adds Uli. "I, on the other hand, really am exceptionally old. I won't go into the sea under any circumstances, rain or shine."

"I've never understood that," says Daniel. "Why are you so afraid of the sea?"

Uli has a recurring nightmare: he watches himself dropping dead in the sea. He's never told this to anyone. Nor does he tell anyone now. He points at Ofélia, who is coming up the ramp, shaking the water from her hair. Abdul waits for her with a towel, eyes fixed on the floor. The poet smiles.

"You are allowed to look at me, Abdul."

Abdul does not. She wraps the towel around her torso, above her chest, and returns to the company of the other writers. It starts to rain. Ofélia remembers the lines of poetry she'd woken up with. She thinks about her grandmother hugging her, she feels her scent, the scent of damp earth, of green grasses, of berries. She says the words out loud, but it's as if to herself:

"All that is liquid calls to me."

"Are you a poet constantly, Ofélia?", says Daniel.

The water is falling more heavily now, but there, beneath the white awning, they are protected. In the days that follow, it will not rain on the island again.

"If you aren't being a poet the whole time, you'll never become one," Luzia replies, pre-empting Ofélia. "Being a poet is not a job, it's a condition."

It is Luzia's youth that makes her stand out from the others. Nevertheless, she gives no sign of being intimidated. She grew up in a house that was frequented by artists and writers, friends of her father's, Camilo Valente, himself a poet, with half a dozen books he'd published during the stormy years of the Angolan revolution. He had been Minister of the Interior, and was now a deputy for the ruling party and professor of African History at the Agostinho Neto University.

Ofélia smiles, like a mother showing her approval of her teenaged daughter. To her, being a poet is like being born with an extra sense – the sense of wonder.

"All poems are a cartography of wonder."

"Assuaging the pain, that's why I do it," murmurs Luzia.

"You talk like a Portuguese writer," Daniel teases. "It's mostly the Portuguese who write because they suffer and suffer while they write. It's like a whole cycle of pain."

Uli laughs.

"Oh, we've all got a bit of Portuguese in us, and a bit of craziness."

"Well, I'm just crazy," insists Ofélia. "I haven't a Portuguese bone in my body."

"'I haven't a Portuguese bone in my body'," Luzia recites, in a serious voice. "'Except the one of this poet's profession.'"

Uli recognises the lines:

"Pedro Calunga Nzagi! The great mystery of Angolan literature . . ."

"The father of us all," says Ofélia.

"Even mine," Uli acknowledges. "He died, didn't he?"

"He didn't die!" Luzia says firmly. "He disappeared."

"How can a ghost disappear?" says Uli, amused. "Has anyone ever seen him?"

"Oh, yes," insists Daniel. "I did a report about him."

"Makes sense," says Uli. "After all, you basically made your name writing about the disappeared and disappearances."

Daniel tells them what had happened. In 1998, the judging panel for the National Literature Prize, in a decision that was very bold, some thought, and very irresponsible, according to others, decided to award the prize to Pedro Calunga Nzagi. They were living through tough times. The war was dragging on forever. The regime was pretending to have become democratised, fraternising with deputies from opposition parties in a sham parliament, while at the same time persecuting the more impertinent journalists. Pedro Nzagi had published his first book of poetry, *Insurgency!*, in 1965, with a small publishing house in Luanda. The book was immediately seized by the Portuguese political police. Half a dozen copies were saved, however, from which hundreds more were made, which would circulate from hand to hand for years afterwards. Nzagi's poetry was read at clandestine evening gatherings. Some pieces were set to music. In 1973, a new title appeared, with a Portuguese publisher, under Pedro Calunga Nzagi's name: *Arson*. This book managed to dodge censorship, winning one of the most important literary prizes in Portugal. Its author, however, did not show up to the award ceremony, nor did he grant a single interview. Five years after independence, a third collection of poems was published, again in Lisbon: *That Wasn't What Was Agreed*. The book provoked a protracted controversy in Angola. Nzagi was condemning the new Marxist regime, in verses that were acidic and ironic and, at the same time, deeply lyrical. Writers close to the regime who had praised him in colonial times hurried to condemn him, accusing him of defending reactionary, neo-colonial ideas. By awarding him the National Literature Prize in 1998, the jury, made up of five young writers, Ofélia Eastermann among them, knew they were provoking the regime's more conservative wing. The following day, the Minister of Culture released a very brusque statement, withdrawing the prize from Nzagi and appointing a new panel. Daniel Benchimol realised he had a good pretext for investigating the life and whereabouts of the mysterious writer. He talked to *Insurgency!*'s publisher, Mario Melo, an old Benguelan freemason, who claimed to have a clear memory of the young poet who, one afternoon, had knocked on his door with a manuscript under his arm: "He was a tall fellow, big, very personable. I was struck by the look in his eye, which was so direct and firm, and even more so by the confidence with which he discussed any subject. At the time he can't have been more than twenty-five, but he talked like somebody who'd lived eighty years already. He was on first-name terms with life. I agreed to publish his book without even having read it. I lost money, of course, because the police collected up and destroyed most of the copies we printed, but I never regretted it." Later Daniel talked to the Portuguese publisher. He, too, remembered the Angolan poet: "A small chap, skinny, rather dull, who handed me his manuscript as if apologising for something. I knew him already, of course, I'd read *Insurgency!*, a legendary book, and I said yes at once." The journalist also talked to three writers, who claimed to have met Nzagi in different places and circumstances. One of them described the poet as a doctor from Moçâmedes, a white man, by the name of Alberico da Fonseco. Another laughed at the first's description: "Nzagi was black. As black as me. He was a maths teacher at the Huambo High School. He died five years ago." The last writer, Rufino Pereira dos Santos, had been a member of the National Literature Prize jury in 1998. He recounted how Nzagi had sought him out, in the middle of the controversy resulting from the awarding of the prize, to thank him for the gesture and entrust him with the manuscript of a novel entitled *The Three Lions*. He was, according to Pereira dos Santos, an elegant mixed-race man of few words. Santos had set up a tiny publishing house, Soyo, which had been publishing very beautiful books that were practically handmade. He was overjoyed at the possibility of publishing *The Three Lions* for the first time, a book that won a number of prizes, in Portugal, Brazil and France. Its author didn't show up at the launches, nor to receive the prizes. There isn't a single known interview of him. No newspaper has ever published his picture. Daniel is convinced that Pedro Calunga Nzagi is a pen-name, and that the man who uses it employed other people to deliver his manuscripts to the publishers.

They are waiting for their dessert to arrive when Jan appears. His hair is wet, down over his forehead, and his shirt is soaked.

"I went for a bike ride. The rain caught me when I was over by the fort. If I was in Switzerland I'd have to change clothes. But it's not worth it here, whatever happens I'm wet all the time anyway, if it's not the rain it's the heat. But I'm not complaining, I like it. So tell me, how's the festival going?"

"The discussions and talks start tomorrow," Daniel explains. "Most of the writers have already arrived. It's all gone smoothly. Just the occasional little alarm, the odd difficult writer."

"Not us!" cries Luzia. "We're the easy ones!"

"Well, since I can eat your tiramisu every night, I'm happy, I don't cause any trouble," said Uli.

"The only person who's complained about our tiramisu was the Nigerian woman," says Jan.

"Well there you are!" says Ofélia. "I believe that's who Daniel was referring to when he mentioned difficult writers."

"I can neither confirm nor deny. By the way, I do need to talk to her. Unfortunately I've got no signal. Do any of you?"

Nobody does.

"The internet's not working either," says Jan. "Must have been the storm."

"So, are we cut off?" asks Luzia. "We really are on an island?"

6

That is how it all begins: the night splitting open in a huge flash, and the island separating from the world. One time coming to an end, another beginning. Though nobody realised it then.

THE SECOND DAY

"What is fire, Antonio?" asked Margarida.
And she herself replied: "Movement."
"Movement?" Antonio was surprised.
"Yes." Hell, meanwhile, seemed to her
a static condition. An apathy. A total tedium.
Before the big bang, before even the word.
But then came matter in movement, and time,
and hell disappeared forever.

DANIEL BENCHIMOL, *Brief History of Fire*

I

Daniel is walking through a city in ruins, his bare feet sinking into the mud, hands pricked by the sharp-pointed grasses, taller than a man. A soldier, beside him, gestures at the tower of an old church, still just about managing to remain standing, bullet-pocked, and says: "There's a flying snake that lives in there." The snake pierces the air, whistling past like a shell, through a forest of trees that bleed and cry and wail, and then Daniel opens his eyes, frightened, and sees a faint glow coming in through the skylight.

He lifts away the sheet, soaked in sweat. Nobody believes in time travel, he thinks, and yet just moments ago he was in Bailundo, in 1996, during the civil war, and now here he is in 2019, in another country, two thousand miles away.

The AC had stopped working. The lamp didn't come on. He remembers why he has no plans to go back to living in Luanda. He'd tired of dealing with the inefficiency of the public services. When there was electricity, there wasn't water. When there was water, the electricity went down. And that was on the good days. On the bad days, there was neither. Rubbish on the streets. The noise of generators making the walls shudder.

On the island, the streets are swept early in the morning, first thing, by hard-working ladies wrapped elegantly in colourful kapulanas. The islanders rarely have to deal with problems with the electricity or water supply. Generators are few and far between, because they're not needed. They'd bought one, thanks to his own stubbornness, but Moira was totally against them. As for water, most of the houses have vast cisterns, built two or three centuries earlier.

Daniel sits up in bed. Moira is sleeping. Her breath sweetens the air. He looks for his phone and checks the time. It's just gone 5 a.m. He still has no signal. No phone network, and no internet. Nothing. He gets up, naked, and leaves the room, careful not to make any noise. Crickets in the yard. The refreshing scent of the vast lemon tree. He leans a wooden ladder against the wall and climbs up to the roof terrace. The sky over the island is clean. There's still the odd straggling star, which has forgotten to follow the rest and is just fading now, as a lazy sun begins to rise below a dark barrier of clouds. The storm makes it impossible to see the mainland.

Daniel remembers what Luzia said the night before. Now, yes, now they really are on an island, surrounded by water on all sides, including above and below, and also by silence and solitude. He gets dressed and leaves the house, heading for the Villa Sands. Uli must still be sleeping. Daniel intends to wake him up.

2

Uli knew it was Daniel even before opening the door.

"It could only be you at this time."

"Did I wake you?"

"No. As you can see, I'm already dressed. I go to bed late and wake up early. I don't even know if I sleep or I just imagine I sleep. I think I've got old."

"Is getting old about not sleeping?"

"Either that, or no longer being able to distinguish between sleep and waking."

"I don't agree, getting old is wanting to sleep."

"I do want to sleep, Daniel. I just can't. In any case, I have definitely got old."

"Well, hey, it seems to work for you, getting old. And it's not me saying that, it's the girls."

"Which girls?"

"Girls, of all ages. I've got ears. I hear what people say."

"Well, none of it seems to reach my ears. Maybe I'm also going deaf. Tell me, is it already possible to get something to eat around here?"

"Not at this hotel, not yet. But I know a roof terrace where they serve delicious toasted sandwiches. Shall we?"

"What about Moira?"

"Moira's asleep, she's young."

3

The terrace of the Café Central Hotel is a kind of secret. Most of the clientele are unaware of its existence. To reach the terrace you cross the lobby, then climb various flights of wooden stairs that lead to the bedrooms. Then you go up one more flight of stairs.

"Amazing terrace!" says Uli, surprised, trying to catch his breath after the climb. "Reminds me of Marrakech."

"You've been to Marrakech?"

"No. I know it from novels. Books have taken me everywhere. Look, there's a guy over there, see? He looks dead."

There really is a man stretched out on his back on one of the cement benches, arms crossed over his chest and a black cap covering his face. Daniel approaches him. He laughs.

"It's Zivane!"

"Is he sleeping?"

"I guess so. Should I wake him up?"

"Nah, he must have been out drinking, yesterday. Is he staying in this hotel?"

"No, he's at the Terraço das Quitandas, with the Nigerians."

"It's good you invited him. His first novel is great and it made some waves, it annoyed a lot of people, which is the best you can ask of a book, but the guy went into a process of slow suicide after that."

"What do you think happened to him?"

"I don't know, I've never understood it. Nor that mad thing of spending years writing the same story over and over, just varying the narrator, I don't get that either. Shall we sit down?"

They choose a table with a view of the sea. The horizon is still hidden behind a dark wall.

"It's raining on the mainland," says Uli. "Raining a lot. Don't you find that weird? It's as if the continent, the whole world, has disappeared."

"Yes," Daniel agrees. "Here on the island it rarely rains. Sometimes we watch the storms, over there on the other side, like they were happening on a distant planet."

A delicate young girl, with deep dark eyes, comes over to ask what they want to eat. There's fried eggs, and bacon, toasted cheese sandwiches with tuna, and yoghurt with cereal.

"What's your name?" Uli interrupts her.

"Pimpinha," replies the girl, fearfully. "Shall I bring the eggs?"

"Bring everything, please," says Uli. "And tell your parents they chose well, Pimpinha's a beautiful name."

Daniel waits for the girl to move away.

"Are you serious? Would you call a daughter of yours Pimpinha?"

"Why not? The only problem is, it'll hardly suit her if she fills out, will it?"

"I wouldn't even give that name to one of my characters."

"When I start writing a novel, it's the names I think of first, and the characters develop out of that. The names determine the characters' personalities. They impose a destiny on them."

"Do you recognise yourself in your name?"

Uli hesitates:

"No. I don't think so. You?"

"No, nor me. If I was one of your characters, what would I be called?"

"You wouldn't be Daniel, that's for sure. Maybe Macário . . ."

"Macário?! For fuck's sake, not Macário."

"Marciano, then."

"Marciano? You're saying I look like a Marciano?"

"You lean forward when you walk, like you want to get there before anybody else. I knew a guy called Marciano who walked like that, all leaning forward."

"What happened to him?"

"To Marciano? No-one knows. He disappeared a few days after independence. He was a lorry driver. A lot of people disappeared in those days. It didn't have anything to do with the way he walked."

"Just as well, I'm relieved. Look, Zivane's got up. He's headed this way."

Júlio Zivane approaches, a little unsteady, trying to protect his eyes, which are being punished by the sun, with the back of his right hand. He leans over the table, poisoning the air with a powerful gust of alcoholic breath.

"If I didn't know you two, I'd think you were only just getting in after a hectic night, with women and a lot of beer." He drags a chair over from the next table and sits down beside Daniel, opposite Uli. "Once you guys've woken up, get me up to speed on what's new."

"We don't have phones, or the internet," Daniel reports. "There isn't any electricity either."

Zivane shakes his head.

"How can you live in a place like this?"

"It's not so bad."

"Isn't Luanda, like, totally *a cuiar*?" Zivane smiles, happy. "I do like the words you guys invent. You Angolans, you're creative."

"I never liked Luanda."

"Does anyone? But seriously, bro, you still didn't have to exile yourself to this back of beyond. Why didn't you go to Maputo? We've read your books, we got a lot of respect for you, a kind of brotherly love, we'd welcome you *maningue* well."

"Moira's from the island."

"Ah, the famous Moira . . ."

"I could live here," says Uli. "Truth is, I do envy this guy."

"No, you couldn't. And this brother-in-law of ours, I don't reckon he'll last long. Don't they say this island is paradise?"

"A lot of people say that . . ."

"Well there you have it. No-one can be happy in paradise. Adam and Eve ran away from paradise."

"Actually, they were expelled," Daniel corrects him.

"That's the winner's version of the story," says Zivane, very seriously.

"Is there any other?" asks Uli. "A Gospel According to the Serpent?"

"That would exist somewhere, but I suspect it's not on sale. In any case, even in the winner's version, it's clear that our venerable ancestors left paradise because they were fed up of the infinite boredom. They chose sin, blessings be upon them."

"Amen," says Daniel.

Pimpinha arrives, having some trouble balancing a tray loaded with everything she had promised. She puts the tray down and passes out the plates.

"Have you got beer?" Zivane asks. "A 2M, really nice and cold?"

Pimpinha goes to fetch the beer.

"Was there some party in this place last night?" asks Uli.

"I have no idea. Where are we?"

"At the Café Central," says Daniel. "You're staying at the Terraço das Quitandas."

"Yeah, that's right, I really like it."

"So what were you doing here?"

"I was sleeping. I would still be sleeping if you two hadn't arrived. You woke me up."

A lot of people like Júlio Zivane because he always says what he thinks. A lot more people hate him for the same reason. Both those who like him and those who hate him are unanimous on one point: Zivane is brave.

Zivane, however, disagrees with those who think this.

While pretending to be asleep, lying on his back on a stone bench at the Café Central, Júlio Zivane made a list of his fears:

Zivane is afraid of the past, which is rather weird if you know that he got his degree in History from Lisbon New University, and that for ten years he was director of the Historical Archive of Mozambique.

It would be, he thought, like a footballer who always ran away from the ball.

Like a baker allergic to bread.

Like an illusionist afraid of illusions.

Also, Zivane is scared of the dark.

Zivane is scared of not being a good father.

Zivane is scared of love.

He is busy with this exercise, listing fears, when he realises someone is approaching. He is very familiar with Uli's voice, everyone in Mozambique knows it well, the warm tone, the gentle way of speaking, with which he disarms his opponents in public debates. They tell stories about the powers of that voice: how one time, while he was trekking in Gorongosa, accompanying a group of English biologists, an old elephant raised his trunk, getting ready to charge, and then Uli addressed him, very calmly, and the animal retreated with head bowed. On another occasion, in Bamako, Uli had persuaded a mugger to lower his weapon and let him continue on his way, chatting to him in Portuguese, a language the mugger did not in fact know. It is also said that the wife of one particular minister asks her husband to imitate Uli's voice when they're having fun in bed, because that's the only way she can achieve a really amazing orgasm. This latest rumour Zivane thinks suspect, or highly exaggerated, since there aren't many men who can imitate Uli's voice. It would be better, the writer had suggested when a friend told him this rumour, to develop a smartphone app, with phrases that Uli would record, for husbands to use when seducing their wives or their lovers.

Zivane doesn't recognise the second voice.

He was ashamed to hear Uli talk about him. Slow suicide. Other people would say "process of self-destruction". Most didn't use elegant euphemisms. They laughed: "Zivane's going to die from all the boozing."

His first novel, *A Refuge in the Camp*, tells the story of a primary-school teacher sent to a re-education camp, right after independence, for having betrayed his wife. It's his father's story. The book, published at the end of the eighties, two years after the death of President Samora Machel in a plane crash, caused some controversy. In those days, almost nobody dared to challenge Machel's legacy. The re-education camps – where, after independence, thousands of people were sent, from women accused of prostitution to young people who liked rock music, wearing bell-bottoms and smoking weed (marijuana, pot, grass, dope, Mary Jane, hash, ganja, etc., because the Devil has more names than God does) – were a taboo subject. Few writers dared to defend the novel. Uli Lima was one of those who did. Zivane felt grateful, all the more so because he had been among those who were criticising Uli at the time, accusing him of using his own stories to mock rural people for their incorrect use of Portuguese.

Júlio Zivane, who was then an employee at the Ministry of Culture, lost his job. He went to Lisbon, with the help of his older brother, Zacarias, and signed up to study History. When he returned to Maputo, five or six years later, the book had stopped being controversial and had become a reference point for younger writers. Everybody was demanding a second novel from him.

Júlio set up a table in the yard, in the shade of a banyan, where his grandfather used to rest, and sat down to write. Zacarias told his friends:

"Júlio's writing again."

Júlio gazed at the fig tree. He saw the birds flying free among the clouds, he saw the sky changing colour, and nothing occurred to him to write but the story of his father, who had died in a re-education camp. He wrote, again, the novel that he had already published, in different words and from a different perspective. In the first book, the narrator was the father; in the second, the head of the camp. He gave it to his editor to read.

"It's the same book!" the man said, annoyed.

"Well, all books about the Holocaust are the same book," said Zivane.

Over the next five years, he wrote *A Refuge in the Camp* seven times. He didn't manage to get any of the new versions published, neither in Mozambique nor in Portugal where the original book was still being reprinted, albeit with diminishing print runs. However, a small French publisher took an interest in the last version, *No-one Prays for Us* (with a plural narrator: all of the prisoners), got it translated and published it. In the six months following publication, nothing happened, not a single review, not a mention on a literary blog, not even one interview request. In the seventh month, a very famous actor recommended the book enthusiastically in an interview on one of the country's most watched TV programmes, and then the reviews and the interview requests did come. The novel sold well in France, attracting the attention of publishers in other countries.

Júlio Zivane could have tried to prolong the brief moment in which the spotlight fell on him, accepting invitations to take part in literary festivals, in writers' residencies and on panels of all kinds, and writing a new novel (a really new one). That was what his agent said.

He didn't do it. He quit his role as director of the Historical Archive of Mozambique. And started a business buying and selling hair. Which is what he still does to this day. He buys hair from India and Brazil and sells it, for extensions, in Mozambique. It's a lucrative business. In any case, as he explains to the journalists who are surprised at his path, it's much more lucrative than history or literature.

The Mozambican had started drinking port the previous night in the company of Jude and Cornelia, the three of them sitting in broad armchairs on one of the verandas of the hotel where they were staying. Leaning back beneath the Milky Way, as though beneath a sleeping god, they started out discussing Sir Richard Burton's translations of *The Thousand and One Nights* and the *Kama Sutra*, and ended up arguing about the differences between Portuguese and English colonialism. They came to no conclusion.

Cornelia Oluokun and Jude D'Souza already knew each other, and, as Zivane quickly realised, they disliked each other politely. They had come from a common tragedy, Jude explained to him, but experienced it in quite different ways.

The Nigerian woman is the main headliner at the festival. She is, moreover, used to being the centre of attention. She arrives and takes over like a storm, asserting herself over everybody, occupying all the space with her brightly coloured boubous, her long braids and the clear laugh of a winner. A tall woman, not only taller than most women but also taller than most men, she dazzles and intimidates.

"There's this idea that being beautiful can be harmful to women's careers as writers, especially when they're starting out," said Jude D'Souza to Zivane, when they were leaving the hotel, because Jude, who had arrived from London that same morning, wanted to see the city asleep. "In Cornelia's case, it wasn't like that. Her beauty helped her to get noticed. And by noticing her, they ended up noticing what she was writing."

"Cornelia writes well," said Zivane.

"I'm not sure what *writing well* is. In any case, Cornelia writes with urgency, which is the most important thing."

"What does writing with urgency mean? If she doesn't write, she'll explode?"

Jude laughed. His walk was brisk, lithe, making the Mozambican jog to keep up.

"She might implode. She writes to change the world."

"I can understand. That's the best possible reason. And you?"

"I wander. I look at the landscape. I'm a landscape writer."

"I think I write to try to forgive."

"I get that. You might implode, too, if you don't write."

"Truth is, I'm in an advanced state of implosion already. I should write more."

Jude came to a stop in the middle of the square. There was no-one to be seen. Not a sound to be heard, apart from the vast murmur of the sea and the distant squeak of an orphan cricket.

"It's like we're alone in the world," murmured Jude.

"That's because we are," said Zivane regretfully.

Jude pulled his Leica out of his leather knapsack and took several photos of the deserted streets. He took a picture of a yellow bicycle leaning up against an old pink wall. He pressed up against a windowpane to photograph, on the far side, the dark face of a Maconde statue. Then, he heard a rough growl behind him, he turned around and saw the dogs. There must have been more than thirty of them, standing there, tense, eyes fixed on the two men. Zivane stood quite still, leaning against a lamp post, as if trying to merge with it.

"So many dogs," whispered Jude. "Where've they come from?"

"What do we do?"

"Stay calm. We'll walk away, very slowly. Just whatever you do, don't run."

At the front of the pack was a Rhodesian ridgeback, large, thin, with feverish eyes, baring its teeth. It took two steps towards Zivane, raised its nose and barked. The writer ran off down the road, not bothering to breathe, much faster than he would have thought himself able. He saw an open door and ran in. He went through, past empty tables, climbed the first flights of steps in one bound, until, not knowing exactly how it had happened, he found himself on the terrace. He walked over to the edge, trembling hard, panting, and peered out onto the street. There the dogs were now, dark and rigid, in a terrible silence, looking at him. No trace of Jude. Zivane lay down on his back on one of the stone benches and fell asleep.

So, what happened to Jude? That's the question Daniel asks when the hair dealer concludes his story. Zivane shrugs. He drinks the rest of his beer. He has no idea. He'd probably gone back to the hotel. Daniel looks for his phone. Still no signal.

"I've got to head over there, to the Terraço das Quitandas. I need to talk to Jude. That's assuming our Nigerian friend wasn't eaten by the dogs. But thirty of them, Zivane, aren't you exaggerating?"

"About thirty, definitely. A vast pack of them."

"There aren't as many as thirty dogs on the whole island," Daniel assures him.

"What do you know?!" Uli laughs. "They could be people

during the day and dogs at night. That happens a lot with us."

"Only in your novels," Daniel teases.

"No," says Zivane. "These things happen."

"Still, I think that's a lot of dogs. Maybe lose about twenty of them."

"Ten. I'll lose ten. There must have been like twenty dogs."

"That's better. Do you guys want to come with me? Jude's speaking this afternoon, at three."

"Oh, I know," says Zivane. "The opening. One of the most anticipated events at the festival. The hall's going to be full. I feel sorry for the moderator."

"I'm the one moderating," says Daniel. "That's why I want to talk to him. So, are you coming?"

4

They find Cornelia on one of the hotel verandas, facing the sea, reading (or rather, rereading) a book by Teju Cole, *Open City*, that she had come across in the hotel library. She stands up, in a whirlwind of colours, and her braids whip through the air. Júlio Zivane does a quick estimate of how much that hair must have cost. A small fortune.

"Good morning!" she greets them, her tone a little acidic. "Finally someone's shown up. What happened?"

"I'm sorry, we've got no network," says Daniel, giving her a hug. "The storm must have brought the lines down."

"Terrible! The phones don't work. I have no internet. I feel completely isolated from the world. I thought there'd been a coup."

"If there has, it hasn't got here yet."

"Everything takes longer to get to this island," says Uli with his gentle voice. "Even time."

Cornelia looks right at him, her eyes shining with mockery.

"Perhaps. The first impression I got when I opened my eyes in the car – because I was sleeping along the way, I slept the whole way from the airport – was of having travelled back in time. Suddenly I was in the nineteenth century. I realised at once that I would not want to live in the nineteenth century."

Uli hesitates:

"Why not?"

"Oh, I couldn't even live in the twentieth. And that's where I'm from. It seems impossible, but I spent my whole childhood in the last century."

"We're all from there," says Zivane. "Specially me, Uli and Daniel. We've come from the very depths of the twentieth century."

"OK, maybe not the actual depths," says Daniel, appalled.

"Oh yes, from the depths, from its very core. We're very ancient. Our Nigerian friend, on the other hand, she's just a girl. I wrote my first novel on a typewriter. There was no internet yet, or mobile phones."

Cornelia feigns astonishment.

"What's a typewriter?"

Jude emerges from the hallway, the skin of his face smooth and glowing, in a crumpled linen shirt, turquoise, hanging down over a pair of black Bermuda shorts. He looks like he's stepped out of a beachwear advertisement. He greets the other writers with a slight nod.

"The light is stunning," he says. "Beautiful morning."

"And the dogs?" asks Uli. "How'd you escape from the dogs?"

Jude frowns.

"The dogs? Oh yes, the dogs. Thirty of them at least. Zivane ran off with them. I came back to the hotel on my own. I'm the kind of guy not even dogs notice. Ever since I was a boy I've suffered from a kind of chronic invisibility."

"Sorry about the internet," says Daniel.

"What about the internet?"

"We haven't got any," Cornelia grumbles. "We haven't even got the phones."

"We have this light, woman! The African sky. The sea, which is so different from ours. Have you ever swum in the Indian Ocean?"

"I need to work."

"We're writers. Our work is absorbing the light, like plants. Transforming the light into living matter. How can you write without first being enchanted yourself?"

"Don't try getting all poet-y with me. Especially not a total social media addict like you. I've heard you make more money from the pictures you put on Instagram than from the royalties from your one book. So are you a writer, a blogger or a photographer, then?"

"I'm all that at the same time."

Daniel coughs nervously.

"Sounds like a good subject for our event this afternoon."

"I thought you were going to be discussing issues around identity and the new Nigerian literature," says Cornelia. "Whatever that is."

"On that we agree," says Jude. "I don't know if there is

such a thing as a new Nigerian literature. I don't even know if there's a Nigerian literature."

"Or if there's a Nigeria?"

"Exactly, I don't even know if Nigeria exists."

Uli laughs.

"The subject that's on the programme doesn't matter remotely. It never does, isn't that right, Daniel?"

"We're just planning to have a good conversation."

"It will be a good conversation," Jude assures him. "Will the audience get to ask questions?"

"Of course."

"Great. That'll be the best part."

"You don't think I can ask good questions?"

They all laugh. Jude waits for them to fall silent again.

"The audience's involvement tends to be more interesting because it entails a certain risk. Moderators are almost always reasonable people, well-behaved. They follow the rules. As for readers, we never know, there might be agents provocateurs in the middle of the audience. Terrorists. It's the unpredictable questions that wake us up, that make us think. They can even get us to give up on ideas we used to be quite sure about."

"I can't give intelligent answers to dumb questions," says Cornelia. "Yes, it does even happen that these terrorists you're talking about can be original, but only because stupidity, sometimes, manages to be original. I've had enough of the idiocy of journalists. Sorry, Daniel, I'm not talking about you."

"I'm not a journalist."

"You're not?!"

"No. I used to be a journalist. Now I'm only a writer."

"Just as well you gave up journalism. That way I can

bad-mouth journalists, specially European ones. There was one time, in Paris, on a really popular TV programme, when this moron wanted to know why, as an African writer, I never put wild animals in my novels."

"I do in mine," Uli admits.

"Maybe because you need lions to make you seem African." Zivane laughs.

"I've got lions in my novels, too."

"I understand Cornelia's annoyance," Daniel intercedes. "For a long time, European critics used to demand that we only wrote about Africa. The Africa they imagined. An African writer who opted, oh, I don't know, to write a novel about the Spanish Civil War would be considered a lunatic. Fortunately that's changed."

Jude, who had sat down on a lounger, facing the sea, turns towards Daniel, surprised.

"Has it really?"

"It's changed so much that you wrote a novel about Lisbon and it was a hit all around the world."

"Fine. Europeans are starting to accept that an African writer is entitled to leave the slave-house and wander the world, just like everybody else. At the same time, if you *want* to deal with lions, why shouldn't you?"

"Because it reinforces the Europeans' prejudices about Africa," says Cornelia, irritated. "Great literature works against commonplaces."

"There are many different realities in Africa and some of them have lions in them," replies Zivane. "I want to write about my country, and there are lions in my country, and magicians, and boys dancing around bonfires. I don't write to please white people, but if white people like my lions, so much the better."

"We shouldn't be so afraid of commonplaces," says Uli. "Every man is a commonplace. Besides, even the most common of places can be totally uncommon. You just need to know how to look."

"Wise words," says Jude, making a slight bow. "The looking is everything."

5

The church of Santo António is bright in the distance, very white, floating like a happy illusion over the polished emerald sea.

Uli stops to look at the setting.

"Is it always like that, the colour of the sea?"

Daniel smiles.

"No, the sea's never the same colour."

"The sea, the sky, or fire. I'm the one who should be living here."

"Don't kid yourself. Zivane's right, you should never trust a paradise. The phrase 'a perfect paradise' isn't a tautology, it's an oxymoron."

Inside the small church, which has been transformed into the HQ for the first Ilha de Moçambique Literary Festival, Moira is leading a restless troop of volunteers. She calls the two friends over and introduces them to a thin young man, with big shining eyes, wearing black jeans and a white shirt, buttoned up at the cuffs. The young man greets them with a short bow.

"So excited to meet you. I'm a big fan of you both. Such different styles, but the same care for ordinary little people."

"Thank you," says Uli. "Nobody's ever said that to me before. What's your name?"

"Gito Bitonga – actor."

"He's the actor who's going to read Jude's text," says Moira, sitting down while supporting her huge belly with both hands. "Each writer will be reading an extract from their respective books at the start of their events. The Nigerians will read in English. Mozambican actors will perform the Portuguese translations. Our friend Gito here takes the job so seriously that he's spent the last twenty-four hours following Jude around, surreptitiously, like a secret agent."

Gito wrings his hands nervously.

"It's the actor's job. I don't just want to be his voice. I want people to believe I'm really him."

"Maybe you should put on a different shirt," Uli suggests. "You look like a priest right now."

"You're only saying that because you haven't heard him read yet," replies Moira. "Gito transforms himself into Jude. If he showed up on the stage dressed as an astronaut, you'd think he was Jude dressed as an astronaut."

6

"'In Portugal there's no racism,' Portuguese people are always saying. Besides sharing this charming delusion, they all think they're white, including two or three unequivocally black people I met in Lisbon."

Gito Bitonga is reading Jude's text in the voice he has stolen from the Nigerian. His gestures are identical, too, the smooth and exact way they slot into one another. The audience is surprised, and starts to laugh. However, they quickly allow themselves to be captured by the text.

"Look at Jude," Uli whispers in Daniel's ear.

The Nigerian writer is leaning forward, his face lit up with amazement.

"If it wasn't for the clothes, I couldn't have told them apart," says Daniel. "The boy's good."

Gito Bitonga continues his reading:

"One night, I was taken to hear fado at a restaurant. On a small stage, a woman was singing. She had short hair, straightened, dyed blonde. When she finished, she came down off the stage and sat at our table. She told me she was Mozambican, born in Inhambane, the daughter and granddaughter of sangomas, though her father was Portuguese, and she called me brother. Then she went on chatting, philosophising about the Portuguese and their congenital sadness. She praised sadness with lovely, firm words. Melancholy is very highly prized in Portugal."

He goes on reading for another fifteen minutes. No sooner has he fallen silent than the audience are on their feet, clapping. Jude and Daniel leave the places they'd occupied, on the front row, and settle into two comfortable armchairs, facing the audience.

"Good afternoon," says Daniel. "It's a great pleasure to be here today, to introduce one of the African writers I most admire, Jude D'Souza. Jude was born in Lagos, in Nigeria, and grew up in London, where he still lives. I'm sorry, I've got to ask you where the Souza comes from, it's such a Portuguese name."

"Boa tarde," Jude greets the audience with a couple of words of Portuguese, before reverting to English, while Moira translates him. "When I got the invitation to this festival, my first reaction was disbelief. I knew Camões had lived in Africa for two years, here on the Ilha de Moçambique, on his way from Goa, and I was curious. I said yes at once. And here I am, here we all are, in the house where maybe he finished writing his *Lusiads*. As for your question, yes, you're right, my name is Portuguese. I'm descended from a Brazilian slave-owner who set up in Benin at the end of the eighteenth century, and made his fortune. He left a lot of children. One of his grandchildren, my maternal grandfather, went to Lagos in search of a woman he'd never met, whom he'd only heard of, and ended up marrying her."

"Was that why, because of that name, Souza, you got interested in Lisbon?"

"I got interested in Brazil first. I visited Rio de Janeiro. I spent eight months in Ouro Preto. I went to Portugal because I'd started writing a novelised biography of that slave-owner great-great-grandfather of mine, Francisco Félix de Souza, and that's where some of his children had studied. Instead, I wrote a novel about Lisbon."

"The narrator of your novel *Such a Dark Light* could be mistaken for the author. Can I call it an autobiographical novel?"

"That narrator's not me."

"He's not? Are you sure?"

"Jude resembles me, we share a similar past, but he's taller, more handsome and much more interesting than I am. Also, he's a jerk."

The audience laugh. The writer notices Daniel's uncertainty and he insists.

"Oh yeah, a jerk. A real son of a bitch."

"OK, a jerk then," says Daniel, while the audience bursts into louder laughter. "That seems a bit of an exaggeration, as a label. Why a jerk?"

"My character, Jude, is a brutally self-centred guy, narcissistic, machista, and misogynist."

"You aren't afraid readers will mix the two of you up?"

"You think I'm a jerk?"

Daniel laughs nervously.

"The narrator of this book has your name, he's a writer."

"I like exploring the possibility of being someone else, someone unlike me, while still being myself. I like confusing readers, too."

The conversation continues. Jude talks about the new wave of African writers, who are more concerned with being writers than with seeming African. He talks about cosmopolitanism, localism and identity. Finally Daniel asks the audience if they have any questions. One girl raises her hand.

"My name's Judite," she says. "I'm a psychology student. Are you married?"

Laughter. Daniel tries to restore order.

"Other questions? Serious ones?"

A tall, solid old man on the back row, with the broad shoulders of an oarsman, his white beard very well kept, stands up. He asks permission to speak English.

"I'm not Mozambican, I've come from a long way away.

I read your novel. I liked it. A jerk, that Jude, it's true. A very nice son of a bitch. A jerk kind of like Hemingway, say. But my question, senhor, isn't about your narrator. What I'd like to know is how you see the future of Africa?"

"Oracles!" sighs Jude. "To a lot of people, we writers are the new oracles. I'm sorry, I can't see into the future. I don't know what's going to happen to Africa."

An uncomfortable silence falls. The old man sits back down, vast and very dignified, on his chair.

Uli puts up his hand.

"Amending the previous question a little: what would a *good* future for Africa be, in your opinion?"

Jude sits back in his armchair, lowers his eyelids and, for a moment, it looks to everyone like he's fallen asleep. Then he opens his eyes and straightens up, looking at Uli directly, ferociously.

"My African utopia?"

"Right, your African utopia."

"Nothing original. I have the same dreams that the first pan-Africanists had: a continent without the bother of borders, independent, alive, free of poverty and corruption."

"That reveals the scale of our failure, don't you think?" says Daniel. "Ours, our generation's. We haven't even managed to create new utopias. On the contrary, we've gone backwards."

7

Uli notices the peeling walls of the old church, on the other side of the road. He has been on the island many times. He has seen that same church almost in ruins before now. He has seen it freshly whitewashed, gleaming in the sun like a bride. The sea makes its way up the coral floor, climbing the buildings, the walls, the bare feet of the children, the women's thick thighs, in such a way that the houses and people also start becoming a part of it. The surfaces of the walls taste of salt. The oldest of the old people are already at least three-quarters sea, one-quarter flesh. If they are able to stand up, on nights when the moon is full, it is due to the strength of their oceanic part. It is the tides that move them.

"I couldn't understand why Jude got so irritated with that old man," says Uli. "Sure, we don't have answers to every question. We aren't oracles. On the other hand, it's true a relationship does exist between literature and magic. We don't always know where certain phrases come from. It happens to all of us."

"The first line is a gift from God," says Luzia. "It was Valéry who discovered that. I don't have that kind of luck. God's never given me anything. So I steal. I steal a lot. I steal lines from poets I love – and even from some I hate but to whom God, in His infinite wickedness, has gifted the odd good line. Basically, I steal from God. No-one who steals from God will go to hell."

They are sitting at a small table on the pavement in front of the Âncora d'Ouro. The two friends are drinking Coke, and Luzia has ordered a beer and some fried prawns.

"Who's the old man?" asks Uli.

"He's Angolan," says Daniel. "He's got an Angolan accent. But I don't know him."

"I thought you knew all our compatriots," Luzia teases him.

"Not all. I'd like to meet this one, though, he seems a very curious character."

"A mystery, then," the young poet concludes, then she adds, "I do love mysteries."

"A mystery, a mystery, that's what's happening here on the island," says Daniel, lowering his voice. "I don't want to alarm you, but since yesterday we've had no contact at all with the rest of the world."

"The internet?"

"Not just the internet. No-one's come in either."

"No-one's come in?"

"No-one's been over the bridge. Yesterday we sent a driver to Nampula, to the airport, to fetch Breyten Breytenbach, and nothing yet. They haven't arrived."

"The road's probably impassable," says Uli. "The car's got stuck somewhere."

"We thought about that. This morning we sent a jeep, with our best driver, a really experienced guy, and he's not back either."

"It's all flooding on the mainland, and out here . . . man, it's this gorgeous night, warm, not even a breeze."

"And what about the sky?" murmurs Luzia, enchanted. "I've never seen so many stars."

8

For several nights, Moira has woken in the middle of her sleep, always from the same nightmare: she sees herself stretched out in bed, in terrible agony, while Lucília, the midwife, tries to contain the torrent of blood and mud that spurts out from inside her. The baby rolls onto the ground, amid crazy-eyed fish and shards of Chinese porcelain, beads, silver coins, while Moira reaches out to it, but the baby slips away and escapes into the blackness of the night, laughing, mocking her.

She is thirty-eight weeks pregnant. She insisted from the very start that she wanted to give birth at home. The father agreed, thrilled. Daniel always bows to her desires. Part of the family, though, continued to pressure her to reconsider her decision. Lucília, who, at first, had shown herself ready to do as Moira pleased, now seemed doubtful. The alternative was to travel to Nacala, where there was a good hospital, but which was an hour and a half's drive away.

Moira sits down on the bed, hugging her belly. She doesn't want to tell Daniel she's scared and that she'd prefer to have the birth in Nacala. Besides, as long as the storm is continuing to punish the mainland, they won't be able to travel.

"Child, be patient a little longer," she says out loud, stroking her belly. "Wait a week, just till the festival's over. Then we'll travel. You can't be born now."

She gets up and fixes herself some tea. The invited writers are complaining because they don't have access to the internet. There's no news of the South African poet Breyten Breytenbach, who was supposed to have arrived in Nampula the previous day. Worse still: they don't know anything about Nampula at all, or about the rest of the country, or about any other place in the world.

As if they didn't have enough problems already, the air conditioner has stopped working. The generator coughs, suffers sharp convulsions. It won't hold out another twenty-four hours. On the island Moira doesn't know a single electrician capable of fixing breakdowns. She tried calling Nampula and Nacala. The phones are still mute. That's fine by her, but Daniel suffers in the heat. He can't sleep. On the hottest nights, a lot of people put mats on the pavement and fall asleep under the stars. Moira would like to do the same, but if she suggested this to her husband, she was sure he'd spend the next few weeks teasing her about it. She can imagine him complaining: "I'm Angolan, an *urban* Angolan. You really think I'm going to sleep on the street, lying on a mat?"

It occurs to her that she could put the bed on the terrace. Up there, even on the stillest of nights, a breeze is always moving. Unfortunately they never got around to installing access steps. Momade de Jesus is in the yard scaling a fish. She watches him finish his job, then asks him to help her dismantle the bed. The servant doesn't seem to find the request strange. He's a serious and silent man, with a bitter past that he doesn't like to talk about. They both kneel down on the bedroom floor, each of them with a screwdriver, and the job is finished in minutes.

"What else do we do?" asks Momade.

"You take all these pieces up to the terrace. We're going to assemble the bed up there. I'll help you."

"Miss is going up?"

"I am."

"Moira, miss, don't do that. It's dangerous. There is no way up, only with the big stepladder or with the wooden ladder. But the wooden ladder is not very safe."

"I know. Please go to my father's house to fetch the stepladder from there."

Momade de Jesus brings the stepladder over, and carries the pieces up to the terrace. Moira goes up, carrying washed sheets and a mosquito net. The two of them assemble the bed. The hardest part is transporting the mattress. They try several different ways. Finally, the man manages to climb the stepladder, one step at a time, balancing the mattress on his head with some difficulty.

"You're my hero," says Moira. "Now pull the stepladder up here. I'm going to need it."

Momade pulls up the stepladder. Moira ties the end of a piece of string to the top of the stepladder and the other end to the satellite dish and uses the structure to attach the mosquito net. Yes, now the bed is ready. It's like a sailboat, very white, ready to sail among the constellations.

"How do we get down?" asks Momade.

Moira laughs.

"I didn't think of that. You can't jump?"

"Jump?!"

"Yes, you jump down to the garden, then you lean the wooden ladder up against the wall and I can go down."

Momade de Jesus shakes his head, in firm refusal. "It's very high."

At this moment, they hear Daniel's voice.

"Moira? Where are you?"

"Up here, on the terrace."

Daniel appears in the yard. He looks up, astonished.

"What are you two doing up there?"

"It's a surprise," says Moira. "You'll like it."

Daniel lies down on his back on the grass, his arms spread, his gaze lost on the darkening sky. He says nothing.

"Seriously," his wife insists. "You're going to like it."

- No answer.

Moira sits down on the terrace, her legs dangling into the void.

"Don't do that," says Daniel, "you could fall."

"Are you angry with me?"

Daniel gets up.

"I'm not angry. I'm worried. How did you get up there?"

"With the stepladder. There's no reason for you to worry. Everything's fine."

"Only we need the other ladder to get down, boss," says Momade. "The wooden one."

"Please don't call him boss," says Moira. "I've told you before, he doesn't like you calling him boss."

Momade looks at Daniel and shrugs. Daniel looks back and responds in kind. Then he goes to fetch the ladder, leans it against the wall and climbs up.

"I can see why you couldn't come back down on the stepladder," he says, admiring the bed, which is standing out against the flaming sky. "If I hadn't arrived you would've been left to live here forever. But yes, I must admit, it does look nice."

"You like it?" Moira hugs him.

"I do. So today we're going to sleep on the terrace, is that it?"

9

Uli loves the sea. But that love notwithstanding, he never goes in. Sitting at the end of the jetty, on the steps that descend into the motionless water, he sees the sun going out on the horizon, the horizon that closes off at his feet like a deep well. He thinks: "There are no happy sunsets." And it occurs to him that he's been through his whole life in a state of sunset. Not through any fault of fate, not that, he had a secure childhood without any major upsets, he likes his job, he's been married forty years, he has children and grandchildren, and he is a well-loved and respected figure in his country. In short, he lacks for nothing.

"Are you sad, Mr Writer?"

Uli looks up. In front of him stands an old lady, very lean and no taller than a nine-year-old child, with a pointy nose and very thin, nervous hands, which seem to be trying to speak for her. To the writer, who has acquired the private bad habit of comparing people with animals, the woman looks like an impossible cross between a chicken and a turtle.

"You find me sad?" asks Uli.

"Oh, always," the woman assures him. "Even when you laugh."

"Thank you for your frankness."

"Nothing wrong with being sad. I always preferred men who were sad."

"Have you come to attend the festival, senhora?"

"My apologies, I didn't introduce myself. My name is Francisca de Bragança. I was born here on the island, many years ago. I've always lived here. I am the last one."

"The last what?"

"Last one in my family."

She falls silent, but her hands continue to move in a frantic dance. "Perhaps it's a sign language," thinks Uli. "I believe that she is in silence yet really she is still talking. It's just that I can't hear her. A person who doesn't know sign language is a deaf person's deaf person."

"Sad men are very elegant," the woman adds. "Happiness, on the other hand, I've always found vulgar. Just look at Rui Knopfli, elegance personified . . ."

"Rui died."

"He certainly did not die!" Dona Francisca laughs. "I talked to Rui this very morning, at the Âncora d'Ouro. He was reading a banned book."

"A banned book?!"

"*Luuanda*, by Luandino Vieira. Have you read it?"

Uli says he has, long ago. Though even way back when he read it, the book had already stopped being banned. He does not say this. He gets up, nods goodbye to the old lady and returns to his hotel.

10

Daniel is at the bar, next to the swimming pool, chatting to Abdul. Uli pats him lightly on the back, taking a seat beside him. He greets Abdul, and asks for a Coke.

"Where have you been hiding?" asks the Angolan. "Nobody heard from you."

His friend shakes his head, with an expression of feigned astonishment.

"You can't imagine what happened to me."

"What was it?"

"Maybe you know a very old lady, very small . . ."

"Dona Francisca?"

"Right."

"You don't need to tell me. I can guess. Did she invite you to a ball at the Governor's Palace?"

"A ball? No, no, she told me she'd spent the whole morning with Rui Knopfli."

"At the Âncora d'Ouro, right? Yes, they're friends, they talk constantly."

"They *used to* talk. Knopfli died in 1997."

"He has died to us, who live in the twenty-first century. He hasn't died to Dona Francisca. She lives in March 1974."

"Always?"

"She does make brief incursions into the present, but she prefers to stay in 1974."

"I get it. She's not a fan of independence."

"Her family left after independence, some to Goa, others to Portugal. The Goan community, or those of Goan origin, practically disappeared. Besides, the island suffered badly from the war and the neglect."

"Oh, I know. When I came for the first time, most of these houses were in ruins."

"They say that ten or twelve years ago, Dona Francisca was knocked down by a motorbike, she hit her head on the asphalt and when she woke up she'd travelled in time, to some day or other in March of '74."

"Always the same day?"

"Apparently."

Uli finishes his Coke and asks for another, with a slice of lemon and a lot of ice.

"It's so hot," he grumbles. "But tell me, if you had to spend the whole rest of your life trapped in one specific day, which day would it be?"

Daniel leans back.

"That's a good question." He shuts his eyes, pensive. "Last week, after lunch, I fell asleep with my arms around Moira. It was, perhaps, the best nap of my life. I could stay in that single hour until the end of time."

Uli laughs.

"Oh come on, you don't need to lie. Moira isn't even here."

"I'm not lying."

"In any case, you didn't answer my question. You have a whole day to repeat, second by second, minute by minute, hour by hour, for the rest of eternity. Which day would you choose?"

"With the exception of the nap, I don't remember what happened that day. Most likely I read, wrote, swam a little, walked the city at nightfall. Yes, I think I'd choose a day like that one, an ordinary day, without any great dramas. A simple day. You know what I wrote in my journal that day? Just two words: lovely nap." He pauses. Then he looks at Uli. "And you?"

"Me?"

"Yes, which day would you like to live in forever?"

Uli opens his arms wide, in mute astonishment.

"Paradise. Because that's what it's about, isn't it?"

"I guess so."

"I do agree with you. Happiness is discreet. It settles itself in and we don't even register it. Then later, when it goes away, we notice that it was there. I hate that cliché, 'I was happy and I didn't even know it,' but I do feel the same way."

"You still haven't answered my question."

"Because I'm so unhappy that I have no answer."

II

Luzia floats, her face towards the night, feeling, at her back, the deepening of the dense darkness of the sea. She allows herself to remain like that, her thoughts adrift, in the hope that the God of poets might grant her a first line. However, instead of a line, the Creator, or whatever it is that plays that role, crouching in the cosmic vastness like a sleepy monkey, sends her a recent memory: "It's all over! Let's salvage what we can: the happy days!"

The young woman straightens up, but her feet don't find the ground. She must be about fifty metres from the beach. She can make out, shining in the moonlight, the T-shirt she left stretched out on the sand. Kiami's words pain her, like a burn. "It was better that way," she murmurs to the vastness, "it was better that way, cutting off the dream before reality could rot it." And then she thinks: "Idiotic, what a stupid line! I'd have preferred to live through the slow process of a dream in decomposition, I'm sure it would have hurt less." She swims towards the beach. Her feet have just touched the bottom again when she notices a shadow detaching itself from the blackness and sitting down beside her clothes. Luzia stops, alert. Then she recognises the shadow, she smiles and moves forward, resolved. She stops in front of the man.

"Why don't you undress and go have a dip yourself?"

Jude looks at her in silence, with a confident, mocking smile.

"I'd rather stay like this, with me very extremely dressed and you gloriously naked."

"Well I wouldn't," says Luzia, looking for her panties and putting them on, her back to him. Then she puts on the T-shirt and a short denim skirt. "I'm going."

"Sit! The night's so beautiful."

"No. The night's strange. And you're being even stranger."

The man kneels up on the sand. He raises his face to breathe in the air.

"You smell good."

"I don't smell of anything. Of the sea, maybe."

"Either that or the sea smells of you." He takes hold of her waist. "In any case, it's a good smell. Let me smell you more deeply."

Luzia shoves him away and he falls backwards, laughing.

"Hey, who's hurt you, woman?"

The young woman buries her fingers in her short braids, shaping them, sticking them out. She lifts her crowned head, her wide eyes gleaming with fury.

"I had a different picture of you," she says, walking towards the road, which is weakly illuminated by a streetlamp. "You should have let me keep that picture."

Júlio Zivane, sitting at one of the tables at Karibu, beside the window, is reading *The Woman Who Was a Cockroach*, by Cornelia Oluokun. Ofélia, who is crossing the road towards the restaurant, sees him put down the book and rub his eyes, as if he has just that moment woken from a strange and uneasy dream. The poet opens the door of Karibu and walks in.

"Good evening, Mister Writer. Have you eaten?"

Zivane jumps to his feet. He points at the chair in front of him.

"Do sit down, Madame Poet. Please sit down. I was killing time. I was just about to ask for the menu. Can I buy you dinner?"

Ofélia sits, arranging the flowers of her dress, smoothing it rather sensually. She smiles.

"I will have dinner with you, Júlio, but we'll each pay for ourselves."

"Is that what things are like in Angola? Because here in Mozambique, it's the man who pays."

"You're wrong. Both in Angola and in Mozambique, sooner or later, one way or another, it's always the woman who ends up paying."

The Mozambican writer looks at her in surprise, then starts laughing, loud, a laughter that seems impossible coming from such a thin and fragile body. Ofélia joins him. They both laugh their fill. Then Zivane points at the book he had been reading.

"Cornelia says something similar, or rather, her narrator does. Guessing you've read it, right?"

Ofélia likes the familiarity with which he addresses her. She had read it, yes. In Cornelia's novel, a cockroach wakes up in a small hotel in Lagos, in Nigeria, transformed into a woman. When she goes outside, she discovers the human world, terribly violent, cruel, incomprehensible. The poet says she finds the book very amusing.

"I think it's scary," admits Zivane. "Actually, a large proportion of the books by new African women writers are scary. This famous black feminism . . ."

"You're not a feminist?"

"No. I'm a traditional African man!"

Ofélia laughs.

"Never say that in Europe."

"That I'm a traditional African man?"

"That you're not a feminist, first of all. And instead of saying traditional African man, say you see yourself as a rightful representative of African ancestral culture. I like your books. And I'm starting to like you . . ."

"I like you and your books, too. I find them scary, but I like them. We can love things that we fear. Truthfully we ought to love only what we fear."

"You're right about that, but I'm not a feminist."

"You're not?"

"No. I'm a bit further ahead. I'm a supremacist. I struggle for a society entirely dominated by women. Or, at the very least, by feminine thought."

"Are you joking?"

"I'm serious. I never joke when I'm talking about women. What is it in my books that scares you?"

"The sex."

"The sex, of course." Ofélia leans forward across the table, coming close to Júlio Zivane's face. The man pulls back. The woman jabs her index finger at his nose. "You should read my first novel, comrade. You'll totally shit yourself."

Ismael interrupts them, to ask what they would like to eat. Immediately afterwards, Luzia appears, and flops unceremoniously onto another chair.

"I've had such an unpleasant encounter."

She describes the episode with Jude. Ofélia thinks it odd.

"What an arsehole! That's not like him at all."

"I've read his book," says Zivane. "Oh, yes, it does sound very much like him, yes indeed."

"Oh for God's sake!" Ofélia gets irritated. "Don't confuse the narrator with the author."

Zivane surrenders.

"OK, don't get angry. You women are all in love with the guy, but maybe he's not the Prince Charming you imagine. Perhaps he's just some poor guy like me, say, a traditional African man. If it'd been me, if I'd been his age and come across a beautiful woman on the beach, and a naked one besides, I'd have tried to get her, too."

"What's this *traditional African man*?" asks Luzia.

"A chauvinist," clarifies Ofélia. "An arsehole."

"Perhaps." Luzia laughs, raising her hand to attract Ismael's attention. "The difference is, at least Jude's handsome."

"Definitely," admits Ofélia. "A bit short, but handsome. As well as elegant and nicely perfumed."

"Hey! I'm handsome, too," Zivane objects.

Ismael presents himself at the table, helpful.

"Have you chosen, miss?"

"What are these two having?"

"Grilled lobster," says Ismael.

"So bring another of those for me." She turns to Zivane. "Handsome, you? Well, that depends on the wine. If they've got some good wine, it could be I'd find you handsome in a couple of hours."

"The wine's good," Zivane assures her, holding up an almost empty bottle. "In vino veritas."

13

Uli looks up and sees a crow detaching itself from the night to fall, silently, onto the rusting metal of the old satellite dish. The bird twists its neck, throwing an intrigued glance in the writer's direction.

"Don't look at me! You'll get a stone thrown at you!"

Daniel – who is climbing the ladder slowly, while his free hand is balancing, with some difficulty, a tray with plates, glasses and two large candles – is surprised by the threat:

"Are you talking to me?"

Uli gets up and goes over to help his friend.

"No. I'm talking to that guy over there, the crow. It's an Indian crow. They're invaders. They arrived from India a few years ago, on boats, and now they're spread across every Mozambican city along the coast."

They put the plates and glasses on the table. It had been Moira's idea. After taking the bed up to the terrace, she decided they'd have dinner there that night, too. Uli, who had known Moira since she was a child, was not surprised.

The two of them sat down and waited for the food to be ready.

"You see?! The guy's still looking at me!"

"Leave the crow in peace," says Daniel. "I never thought I'd hear you ranting against immigrants."

Uli laughed.

"They attack the indigenous birds, they eat their eggs. They destroy everything."

"It really does sound like a xenophobic diatribe."

The crow comes down onto the terrace. It remains motionless a moment, distrustful. It approaches the two friends with cautious hops, its curious eyes, very ancient, fixed on Uli's blue irises.

"Those eyes of his!" Daniel is frightened when he sees the moon setting inside them. "The light in his eyes."

"They're very intelligent animals," says Uli. "We tend to distrust clever animals that don't look like us. Gorillas, well, they're fine, they're close cousins. But we find it hard to accept that octopuses or crows can be intelligent."

The crow circles slowly, never taking its eyes off Uli, then it greets him with a silent nod, takes flight and disappears into the darkness. A long lightning-flash illuminates the terrace. They hear Moira calling, from the yard. She has put the pan with the food into a straw basket then tied a rope to the handles. She throws the free end of the rope up onto the terrace. Daniel manages to grab it on the first attempt and pulls the basket up. Moira climbs the ladder. They light the candles, then serve themselves matapá de siri-siri, a traditional island dish made with a local mangrove plant, and cassava xima.

"If I had to choose the top five dishes of traditional cuisines, from all the countries I know, I'd put your matapá in first place. This one in particular, it's really very good," says Daniel. "What I cannot accept is your style of funje."

"He says our xima has sand in it," Moira complains.

"It's true, you don't sieve the bombó flour. Or if you do, then you sieve it badly."

"Daniel's right," Uli agrees. "But you're not supposed to chew the xima. You swallow it, sand and all. It's good for you."

"Sand's good for you?"

"Exceptionally. When I was small I used to run away from home to eat earth. If you gave me a bit of earth, I could tell you if it was from our yard, the neighbour's yard or the open land by the river."

"You had a refined palate for earth?" Moira teases him.

"I still do. I've even thought about opening a restaurant that only serves earth. Earth from various countries: the best hard mud from Beira, humus from the Nile, sand from Ipanema, the sacred mud from the Ganges."

The idea is received with laughter. They spend several minutes discussing what name they're going to give the restaurant. The shadows thicken while they eat. Moira tells the story of an Englishman who used to go around in dark glasses, at night, on the island, because he couldn't handle the splendour of the stars.

14

Cornelia Oluokun, stretched out on a charpai, on a terrace that is so white that, even at night, its whiteness shines, is contemplating the eternity that weaves a fine web of silence around her. She sees Jude's shadow approach. She doesn't move. The other writer sits down on the chair beside her.

"Calmer?" he asks.

"More reconciled. It's as if we've died."

Jude considers the possibility.

"Could be. I imagine the dead don't receive news from the world of the living. And the living, do you think they know about us?"

"The living have forgotten us already."

"Me definitely. You, I doubt it. You're hard to forget."

Cornelia turns her head towards him.

"Is that a compliment?"

"It's the truth."

"I thought you didn't like me."

"You're wrong. I do and I'm a great admirer of your work."

"I read your review of my second novel. I didn't get the sense you liked it." Cornelia sits up straight and imitates Jude's posh accent. "Yes, Cornelia Oluokun's new novel begins well, with a spark of genius, but that is not enough to illuminate seven hundred pages of a prose that is dense and not always elegant."

"Did I write that?"

"You did."

"If I remember rightly, I gave it four stars, out of five."

"Precisely. You did not give it five."

"I am sure I have never given any novel five."

They fall silent. Cornelia lies back on the charpai. She regrets having spoken. On the other hand, she's had that thing jammed in her throat for months, poisoning her. Now finally it was out. Tomorrow she'll feel better. Jude considers telling her to go to hell, getting up and going for a martini at the bar of the Villa Sands. He lets it be. He doesn't want to fall out (perhaps forever) with the writer who is favourite to nine out of ten cultural journalists. *Time* considers her one of the most influential women in the world. It is said that she received a million-dollar advance for the US edition of her next novel. A novel that is not yet written, doesn't even have a title, but of which it is said that it might come to be "the second de-colonisation of Africa" (*The Times Literary Supplement*). So he would rather change the subject:

"What's your panel about, tomorrow, the one with Uli Lima Levy?"

"Literature and feminism."

"You're not serious!"

"No, of course I'm not serious. I would have refused. In any case, it's an equally idiotic subject: 'The enemy gaze'."

"Doesn't sound idiotic to me," replies Jude. "The point is to discuss literature's capacity to let us see other perspectives, sometimes antagonistic ones. Your books do that very well, and Uli's do, too."

"What have you read of his?"

"I've read all the novels that have been translated into English. I'm reading the new one in Portuguese now. Actually, that's what I've been doing these last few hours, sitting on my veranda, with the help of a Portuguese-English dictionary."

"And?"

"I'm finding it really interesting. It's got this real joy in fable-making, something that's been lost from a lot of contemporary European literature, but not here, not in Africa. As a general rule, we do still like telling stories. You've got that quality, too.

Uli's book seems to rest upon an autobiographical foundation, we're led to believe that the boy was him, fifty years ago, but then something happens that just dynamites rationality. It's actually nothing to do with auto-fiction. I hate auto-fiction."

"Your book is pure auto-fiction."

"It's not, it's a parody of auto-fiction. In any case, I hate my book. Why do you think I still haven't published another? Because I don't want to write and publish the same stupid book. I want to do something totally different. I just don't know what that'll be."

15

Five years earlier, Daniel had woken up not knowing where he was and he thought he was surrounded by a myriad of small silver creatures, which flitted past him, through the darkness, just centimetres from his face. Then he remembered he was in the cabin of an ocean liner, sailing between the Greek islands, and he sat up, dizzy, his naked body leaning against the broad windowpane, waiting for his sleepiness to dissipate. That, however, did not happen. "Maybe they're birds," he thought. But they couldn't be birds. Not at night. Not like arrows pointed at the heart of time, smooth and shiny and with large moonlit eyes. They were fish. Thousands and thousands of flying fish.

At the exact moment he wakes up, on the terrace, Daniel has been dreaming of the flying fish. Moira is asleep, head resting on his chest. A crow – perhaps the same one that had visited them before dinner – is wandering along the cord holding up the mosquito net. They exchange a look like a pair of spies who, never having seen each other before, recognise each other among the crowd. "I know what you are," say the crow's mocking eyes.

Daniel remembers the afternoon he met Moira. He had gone to visit her in Cape Town, because he wanted to have a look at her work as a visual artist. At the time, Moira was devoting herself to staging and photographing her own dreams. They talked about Luanda, where Moira had lived as a teenager, with her father, who had been hired to run an Angolan civil construction firm. Unlike Daniel, the woman retained good memories of the city.

"We danced a lot," she told him. "I've never danced as much as I did in those days."

They discovered they had friends in common. Perhaps they had met at one of these friends' flats, at a Saturday lunchtime funje, without either of them noticing the other. At the turn of the century, Moira, then seventeen, went to study photography in London. A year later, she moved to Rio de Janeiro. Around the same time, Daniel also traded Angola for Brazil, tired of losing battles. They concluded, having done the sums, that during this carioca phase they would again have been very close on several occasions: at a carnival party, at the artist Adriana Varejão's flat; at a Gilberto Gil show; at the launch of one of Uli's novels; at the preview of an Andrucha Waddington movie; at a tribute to the Mozambican poet and movie-maker Ruy Guerra. Later, in October 2005, Daniel had visited Ilha de Moçambique, the island also called Muhipiti, on a research trip for one of his novels. Moira was there, on holiday, based in the only hotel operating at the time: the Muhipiti.

"You know the joke about the guy who got caught in a terrible flood, who climbed up onto the roof of his house to wait for God to help him?" Daniel had once asked Moira. Moira hadn't heard the joke before. "Well, the guy was really devout. So he went onto his terrace, and as the waters rose, he knelt down, praying to God to rescue him. A fisherman appeared in a canoe and invited him on board. 'Thank you very much,' the man said, 'but there's no need, the Lord God will save me.' The water continued to rise. Two hours later, a firefighters' boat came past. They climbed onto the terrace and tried to get him off, but he squirmed loose and pushed them away: 'No! I trust in the Lord God, He will come to save me.' Finally, with the water already overtaking the terrace, a military helicopter flew overhead. The man, however, insisted on staying, waiting for God to help him, and so he drowned. The moment he found himself face to face with the Creator, he protested: 'I have always believed in You, and yet You couldn't save me!' God got annoyed: 'I sent you a canoe, I sent you a boat, I sent you a helicopter – and you refused them all? I can't stand idiots!'"

Moira laughed.

"Why did you just remember that?"

"Because I also spent years asking my late grandmother, who is my protector, and who is my guide, and to whom I pray, to send me the woman of my life, and I always thought she was playing deaf. Turns out I was the one who was blind after all."

Moira thought his approach impudent and arrogant. On the other hand, she did feel flattered. In Brazil, a friend had lent her Daniel's first novel, but she hadn't liked it. "It's boring and pretentious," she said when she returned it. Some years later, when she had settled in Cape Town, she read it again and it was like a different book. She had laughed. She had cried, very moved, on discovering that the narrator of the novel was her herself, in a past in which she had never lived. She had thus discovered that nobody reads the same book twice. A little later, she would understand that nobody reads the same books – even reading the same books. So, what Moira said, after the initial shock, was:

"Tell me about your grandmother."

Four months later, they were living together in Lisbon. Moira wasn't handling the winter well. She hated coats, scarves, boots, any sort of clothing that impeded her movements. She had lived for too long far from Africa, which to her included those years in Cape Town. "It's not really an African city," she tried to explain to Daniel, "it's a Europe in exile."

She wanted to go back to feeling herself, that is, to laughing loudly in public places, without the fear that somebody looking might find her odd; to wearing kapulanas, leaving her breasts loose inside; to swimming in the hot waters of the Indian Ocean.

She dreamed of her father's land. She had only seen the island for the first time after the end of the war. From the first time she crossed the narrow three-kilometre bridge, she felt this was her place. In the interim, her father had recovered the old family mansion, and she thought that, if she hadn't been born there – she was born in Maputo – she could at least try to be *re*-born. That process of rebirth included having an islander child.

Daniel got to know the island through the poetry of

Camões, Alberto de Lacerda, Rui Knopfli, Luís Carlos Patraquim, Nelson Saúte and so many others, all of them praising the historic tradition of miscegenation of the town where, for centuries, Arabs, Swahilis, Makuas, Portuguese and Indians settled; some of them Muslim, others animist; some Hindu, others Christian; and even a radiant mixture of them all.

On that first visit, in 2005, the Angolan writer rediscovered a part of his own childhood, in the large, deep, perfumed backyards, where banana and papaya trees grew, or in the slow heavy numbness of the afternoons. It occurred to him that he might buy a ruin. And so when Moira suggested they go to live on the island, he agreed enthusiastically.

For centuries Muhipiti has been split down the middle, into the town of stone and the town of macuti, the name given to the strips of flattened palm leaves used to cover the wattle-and-daub houses. The city of stone and whitewash – where the colonial mansions are, the main churches, the courthouse, the spacious and beautiful São João de Deus Hospital and the São Sebastião Fort – was constructed out of the coral stolen from the other part.

So the half where the poor live is now stuck inside a huge hole. Today the impression you get from this division is even more unpleasant, because almost all the old houses of wattle-and-daub and macuti, which, though humble, did at least boast a certain nobility and elegance, were replaced with cement-block shacks, with zinc roofs, on which horrible satellite dishes sprout like metallic mushrooms.

Daniel sits up on the bed. The movement wakes Moira.

"What are you thinking about?"

The man doesn't move.

"About death."

"About death?!"

Daniel turns towards her.

"Imagine you bring a baby elephant here onto the terrace . . ."

Moira laughs.

"Why the hell would I bring an elephant onto the terrace?"

"Well, if you brought a bed, you're capable of bringing anything, so just make that bit of effort and imagine you bring an elephant."

"OK. I can see an elephant on the terrace . . ."

"Great. In the first few months, the animal's small, it runs around the patio. Then it grows. It can hardly move. Finally it becomes motionless. Right?"

"Right!"

"I think the same thing happens to time, when it's kept inside you. The years multiply and they end up occupying everything. Then, time stops. You look inside yourself and you see the countless moments, all of them motionless, every second of your life totally static, and you go back to feeling the joy or the sadness you experienced when you were going through them. That state, when time stops growing inside us, is what we call death."

Moira lies back down. She yawns.

"Oh, for the love of God! Spare me the philosophy at this time of the morning!"

She falls asleep again quickly. The crow jumps down from the string onto the ground. It tries a few little hops around the bed. It moves away and immediately returns, as if wanting Daniel to follow it. The writer pushes the mosquito net aside.

He gets up, naked, and goes after the bird. It jumps onto the neighbouring patio and from there twists its head, challenging him. The man follows it. His father-in-law had told him that, seventy years ago, he and the other kids used to cross the stone city from end to end, running along the walls and terraces. On some blocks, where most of the houses have been restored, this is once again possible. The crow jumps across to a third terrace, and then to a fourth. That one overlooks a small internal courtyard, in ruins, covered up to the throat with leafy banana trees.

In one of the corners there's a cement bench. Jude is sitting there, next to a tall, lanky man, with a kapulana tied round his waist and his face painted white. Daniel recognises him: Baltazar, the island's tramp, who likes wandering around at night dressed as a Makua woman. His face, with its pointy nose and wide, engrossed eyes, always protected by mussiro – a white paste obtained by macerating a root, which the Makua women put on their faces to protect and beautify their skin – reminds you of a distracted ghost. Some people are afraid of him. Most ignore him.

The two men, Jude and Baltazar, are in silence, not looking at each other, but it seems to Daniel as though they are sustaining an intense conversation. Then, Baltazar looks up and the Angolan writer sees that his eyes have within them the same gleam (the same spreading moon) that he found in the crow. Frightened, he flinches back, trips over his own feet and almost falls. On his way back home, running like a little boy across the centuries and the terraces, he hears, quite distinctly, Jude D'Souza's mocking laughter.

THE THIRD DAY

Michele has left this strange world a little before me. That means nothing. People like us, who believe in physics, know that the distinction between past, present and future is no more than a persistent and stubborn illusion.

ALBERT EINSTEIN, in a letter to the sister of Michele Besso at the time of his death, on 15 March 1955. Einstein would die a month later.

I

"She looked at herself in the mirror, anguished. The world had shrunk. She, meanwhile, was enormous, struggling to balance on her hind legs, while the front ones leaned on a wall. She really missed her middle legs. Moreover, without the hard chitin exoskeleton, she felt fragile, exposed, terrified at the possibility that at any moment something might appear and crush her. She opened the door and went out into the hallway. She mustn't see anybody, not the way she used to be, and not the way she was now. She walked across the corridor, went through another door and into the lobby. There was a man sitting behind a small desk. He got up when he saw her, and the woman thought he was about to start yelling, that he would come towards her and try to tread on her. The man, however, merely smiled as he asked: 'Do you feel alright, madam?' She was a woman, then. She was one of them. And she felt alright. She felt really very well indeed. She straightened up and headed out to the street."

Ofélia Eastermann takes off her glasses, looks up and explains that she has just read an extract from the first chapter of Cornelia Oluokun's *The Woman Who Was a Cockroach*. She will next read two more extracts, one from the sixth and another from the ninth chapters, hoping that these might arouse the audience's curiosity. Anyone who wishes to purchase copies of the book can head for the stall that has been set up next to the bar. She puts her glasses back on and continues to read.

In the sixth chapter, the woman who was a cockroach reveals her perplexity when faced with the various conflicting religions of humanity: "They kill each other, or allow each other to die, in the cruellest ways, in the name of fantastical beings, who are utterly oblivious to the fates of the creatures that revere them. [. . .] She could see no virtue in mankind except as producers of very fine garbage. [. . .] They seek God the same way cockroaches seek garbage, but those few who find it (if they find it) do not enjoy it."

Finally, the woman who was a cockroach finds a man, Max, to whom she can relate, somebody as horrified by humanity as she is. The two of them travel various countries, in search of a place where they can return to a utopian life in the world of synanthropic insects. In the ninth chapter, they are wandering the streets of a small fishing village, on the east coast of Mexico, when an old indigenous woman approaches them, looks directly at the woman and recognises her: '*La Cucaracha!*' she says. There is no alarm in her voice, and no repugnance. On the contrary, the announcement is a happy one. 'We've been waiting for you for so long!' The next morning, the couple wakes on the beach, in the inaugural light of a blemishless sky. The sky is floating down amid a labyrinth of rocks. The breeze carries the good smell of rotten algae.

There is faint, disjointed applause.

"I don't think they liked it," Júlio whispers in Daniel's ear. "They're scared."

On the stage, sitting beside Uli Lima, Cornelia Oluokun illuminates the hall with the vibrant flames of a lacy red dress, which, on her body, seems an insult to every other less elegant woman. Sitting in the third chair, the moderator, the Brazilian journalist Jussara Rabelo, cannot take her reverent eyes off Cornelia's face. The first question, addressed to the Nigerian woman, is not very original:

"Has exile changed the way you write?"

Cornelia was born in Lagos, but she has lived since adolescence in New York. She returns to Nigeria every year to visit relatives and friends and also, she adds with a radiant smile, to "gobble up sun by the slice and listen to people". If she had never left the country of her birth, she might not be a writer. She started to write as a means of resistance against forgetting and denationalisation, because she was afraid of stopping being Nigerian, and continued because she discovered the simple pleasure of telling stories and because writing became a part of her identity. Today she doesn't feel like a foreigner in New York. She feels like a New Yorker who happens, by chance, also to be Nigerian, and she sees no conflict whatsoever in this.

"Can we think of your book as a tribute to Kafka and to the whole canon of great Western literature?"

"You can think whatever you like." Cornelia is exasperated. "Any novel, if it's good enough, pays tribute to dozens or hundreds that came before it. In my library, as in life, I do not divide up my books according to the nationality of their authors. I don't ask people where they're from. What I want to know is who they are. Then I ask them what they like reading."

"And yet it is a possible way of dividing up, this question of the library," Jussara presses her. "How do you organise yours?"

"By colour of spine. Red, orange, yellow, green, blue . . ."

The audience laugh. Cornelia notices the interviewer's torment and apologises, smiling. She points at Uli Lima.

"Aren't you going to ask our other writer any questions?"

Jussara gets flustered.

"Yes," she says, "of course." She consults a small notebook and finally moves on to the subject of their discussion: "We've just heard extracts from your new book, *The Drowned City*, which seems to contain many autobiographical elements, and from the trilogy *The Crocodile Conclave*, a historical novel, in which you posit an African look at Portuguese colonisation, while at the same time making an effort to understand the Europeans' point of view. Which of these is harder for a writer: exposing yourself, or trying to see the world through the eyes of others, and ultimately, perhaps, the eyes of the enemy?"

Uli Lima greets the audience. He tells a joke, recalls a traditional Makua tale, and within minutes he has won his listeners over. The moderator suspects he hasn't answered her question, but realises that this doesn't much matter. The rest of the session passes amid much laughter, with the writers exchanging stories to illustrate different points of view. Cornelia even dares to sing an old Yoruba lullaby, which she learned from her maternal grandmother. Jussara Rabelo, who is on her first visit to Africa, the continent where her ancestors were born, is overcome by emotion, leaving the stage in tears. The audience rises to its feet to applaud.

2

Resting on the head of Luís de Camões, the crow watches the square. That is its territory. It was born there, fifteen years ago, in the ruins of a vast mansion, where a fabric store operated in colonial times, the property of an Indian trader. The building went up at the start of the nineteenth century, on the ruins of an old mosque, built by the Portuguese poet Tomás António Gonzaga, who had been exiled to the east coast of Africa for plotting in Minas Gerais against the Portuguese crown's rule. The poet was happy in Muhipiti. He married the daughter of a wealthy slave-owner, a delightful, happy girl, who despised poetry and politics. They had two children. Today, there are many Mozambicans proudly boasting the poet's surname. A whole mixed-race legion.

The crow has no awareness of history. It was born amid the rubble. Its upbringing was spent tearing pieces of wrapping paper, ledger books, black and white photos of three generations of the Alibay Jamals. One morning, pecking at the thick walls, it found silver coins. But it could find no use for them. Later, it witnessed the restoration of the building. In disgust, it attacked the foreman, which resulted in three of its children dying from poison. From time to time, the old crow still flies up onto the roof tiles, and then, shutting its eyes, it feels its little heart tighten with anguish.

Currently it is busy crapping on the head of Luís de Camões, its eyes half-closed in pleasure. It hears a hoarse cough behind it. Turning its head, it sees an old man, very tall, very solid, walking around the pedestal with an energy uncommon in his age. The old man rests both hands on the marble plaque bearing the name of the author of *The Lusiads*. Looking up, he spots the crow.

"Ah, dear poet, such misfortune, to be represented here so preposterously and serving as a latrine for the sons of bitches crows."

Even though he doesn't know what a son of a bitch is, the crow can sense from the tone that it is no compliment, and with an enraged caw, it takes flight up into the ragged branches of a casuarina tree, a few metres away, from where it continues to watch the square. The old man sits down on one of the cement benches set into the seawall that protects the island from the water, he stretches out his legs, takes a book out of a leather knapsack, opens it and begins to read.

A young woman approaches. She is wearing denim trousers with wide rips on the knees and a black T-shirt bearing the words, in white letters, "We are the granddaughters of the witches you couldn't burn". Her hair, sticking out in little braids, gleams as if it has been waxed. She stops in front of the bench, studying the old man. He looks up and smiles.

"Was there something you wanted?"

"I think I might know you."

"I'm sure we've seen each other around. The island's small."

"No. I know you from somewhere else, senhor. Are you Angolan?"

"Didn't you hear what Cornelia said this morning?"

The girl laughs.

"Right. So – what are you reading?"

The old man shows her the cover of the book: *Ghana Must Go*, by Taiye Selasi.

"The correct question, according to Cornelia, would be

'What do you *like* reading?'"

The girl sits down next to him.

"Very well. I'm impressed. So tell me: apart from African literature written by women, what other subjects appeal to you?"

"The history of mindsets, etymology, ornithology, old cartography, poetry. I've always read a lot of fiction, but lately I've been more interested in the dead: Machado de Assis, Eça de Queirós, Clarice Lispector, García Márquez, Borges, Cortázar, Nabokov, Kapuściński. And as for poetry, what really excites me is the most alive there is. I've read your books, young Miss Valente. May I call you Luzia? In the first, you were seeking your own voice. It's possible to make out other presences in those lines, not all of them good. Some of them, frankly, did deserve the solace of being forgotten. But the following books, I'll admit it, surprised me. They brought me huge happiness."

Luzia looks at him, intrigued.

"Ornithology?"

"Yes . . ."

"Cartography?"

"Yes . . ."

"Including maps of imaginary cities?"

"Yes, I like them very much."

"Do you write, senhor?"

"Sometimes. When I forget myself."

"You published a book about a man who drew maps of non-existent places. As he drew them, these places began to exist. Birds were born in them."

"You must be mistaking me for some other writer."

"You are Pedro Calunga Nzagi!"

"Who?"

Luzia kneels on the asphalt.

"Master! I don't even know what to say . . ."

The old man takes her hand, forcing her to sit back down. Luzia hugs him. She cries.

"Reading your books, master, it was like living through an earthquake."

The giant smiles, ill at ease.

"Please, enough of this 'master' business."

The young woman wipes her face with her T-shirt.

"As a child, and, later, when I started to get interested in poetry, nobody talked about you, senhor. People used to hide your books. Your name was banned."

"Very sensible measures, let's face it."

"Don't laugh. It's not funny. I discovered one of your books by chance, hidden behind others, in the garage. I was seventeen. I read it right there, my heart pounding. I took it inside. I remember it all so clearly, Saturday, late afternoon. My father in the living room, watching the football. I burst in, yelling, waving the book, like somebody who had just witnessed a miracle. Then he got up from the sofa, took the book from me and started tearing out the pages, ripping them up. Dancing about like a thing possessed while he trod on the pages that had fallen on the floor. Honestly, senhor, can you believe it?"

The old man stands up. He turns towards the sea, leaning on the wall with his strong hands. He knows very well who the young poet's father is. He can imagine the scene. He remembers the first time he saw Camilo Valente. The future Minister of the Interior can't have been more than eighteen, and it was already possible to see in him the great virtues and the solid deformities of character that would be consolidated later, transforming him into one of the key pillars of the party. What Camilo did was to place three or four innate qualities – determination, courage, discipline – in the service of certain moral failings, in particular an excessive ambition. Men entirely without qualities rarely become dangerous: they are merely useless. The dangerous ones are those who use certain qualities to strengthen their wickedness. Camilo distinguished himself, in the days of the clandestine struggle, as a good militant, who didn't hesitate to fulfil the toughest missions. After independence, he revealed an almost magical talent for navigating the dangerous waters of revolution, managing to remain always on the side of whoever won. He received, thanks to this powerful intuition, the nickname Kimbanda, which irritated him tremendously at first, but which, as the years went by, he would end up accepting and adopting.

The old man turns to Luzia.

"Thank you," he says. "Thank you for your books and for your joy. Have you already seen the mangrove, here on the island? I'm always amazed when I see the beauty springing up from the mud, life organising itself from out of death."

The crow, who has followed the whole scene, hopping from branch to branch on the casuarina, cannot tell whether this has been a first meeting or a reunion.

3

Seated in the bath, with the water falling, steaming, onto her naked body, Cornelia cries. She couldn't have said for sure why she does. She had returned to the hotel alone, right after her panel. She tried calling home. She needed to hear Pierre's voice. The telephone, however, was still mute and the internet was dead. She feels alone. She had agreed to take part in the festival on her agent's insistence. "It's an African event," Muriel had reminded her. "There are so few of them. Your presence would be a big deal for them. And besides, you might get some idea or other for the new novel."

Cornelia met Pierre Mpanzu Kanda in Paraty, in Brazil, at a literary festival. When she learned that she would be sharing her event with a Congolese writer, she got irritated: "So we're the Black people's event?" The organisers got very nervous, insisting no, no, they'd decided to bring the two of them together owing to their similar paths: her, Nigerian and American; him, Congolese and French. They could talk about multiple identities. The writer agreed, though she remained sceptical. Contrary to all expectations, she had a lot of fun at the event, she laughed, she was moved. The audience gave them a five-minute standing ovation. They spent two hours signing books. At the end, Pierre invited her for a drink at one of the historic town's many bars. By that point, she was already in love. The Congolese man was like a surfer: tall, strong shoulders, square jaw, healthy-looking, with gestures that were confident and calm, and the distantness towards life's urgencies of some-one who's on holiday in life. It wasn't an easy romance, as Pierre was married to a French publisher, a situation that continued for another two years, before he finally divorced, moving, with all his books, his silk shirts and his made-to-measure jackets and trousers, from Paris to New York.

In the bath, Cornelia thinks about the conversation she'd had with Jude the previous day. Maybe it's true, maybe she is dead and she's now in hell – because what else could you call this damn island? A narrow, closed-off, crude place, far from everything she loves: her husband, her books, music, theatre, museums and galleries, good restaurants, the parties she's always throwing in her apartment, the streets filled with crowds, in New York, London, Paris or Lagos; the dinners with interesting people from the world of arts and politics; the teas with her girlfriends to hone their gossip.

What has she done to deserve hell?

Then she thinks about the new novel. Everyone is pressuring her: Muriel, the publishers, journalists, literary critics, her friends, even Pierre. In a foolish impulse she'd told a journalist that she was writing about the rebirth of Africa – a big novel, a huge novel, telling the story of a Nigerian family from the mid-nineteenth century up until 2050. "Are you making progress?" the journalist wanted to know. Oh yes, she replied, she'd already written almost three hundred pages. All because that morning, leafing through some books she'd bought in Paris, from an antiquarian book dealer, she'd found a postcard dated 1900, showing three Senegalese lads, very well dressed, with the caption "*Thiès – Trois Élégances Masculines*". At home, her husband had hugged her: "A new novel? And you never mentioned it to me? Let's celebrate." Cornelia didn't have the courage to tell him the truth, not even when, that night, he took her out to his favourite Ethiopian restaurant and flooded her with questions. She shut herself away at home writing. She focused on the image of her grandfather, an old gentleman she'd barely known, but from whom she had inherited an iron walking-stick with the symbol of Oxum. She knew that, if she could just create the family patriarch, he would generate all the other characters, with their private dramas, their aspirations, their fears and failings, and the novel would start to flow. After a month, however, she had written only thirty weak pages. The patriarch was an elusive shadow, stretched out on his deathbed, with no name of his own, with no strength, with no past to justify the future of a whole large and prosperous family.

She abandoned the fading patriarch on his sad bed, and began to write another novel about a young Nigerian prostitute, who was involved with a corrupt and violent politician. Lola, the prostitute, yes, she grew fast. Cornelia was on page 55 when *The Times Literary Supplement* ran a piece that mentioned her next novel: "An ambitious family saga, written with the vigour and irony we have come to expect from Oluokun, but even more innovative: the second decolonisation of Africa." Pierre arrived home waving a copy of the paper, and came into her study without knocking (Cornelia had put a sign on the door: "Do not disturb: genius creating ideas") and shouted, while yanking her up from her chair into a delighted hug: "So how's this great family saga of yours going?"

The moment he left, Cornelia called Muriel: "What have you done?" The agent had been expecting the call. She tripped over herself with apologies. The journalist had been very insistent. Besides, the publishers, who had already paid significant advances, did want some news of the novel. She had just thrown them a few peanuts. She'd told them she had read the first thirty pages and been really impressed. She'd said the same thing to the guy from the *TLS*. "This isn't bad for you, on the contrary," she assured her. "The piece came out today and I've already had two calls from publishers interested in the novel, one in Japan and one in India. What you need to do is just write. Just write, honey, write, this book's going to be huge."

Cornelia cannot write the novel they are expecting from her. And now here she is, in the arse-end of hell, getting slow-cooked in a steamer, while all around her, people laugh and chat about the little mishaps of life, happily oblivious to the fact that they are dead.

4

Uli Lima Levy, sitting by the pool, dangling his feet in the water, is following the dogged progress of a small boat, laden with nets and fishermen, that is skirting past the deck. Daniel says that he saw Jude last night, in the company of Baltazar, but his friend ignores him. He remarks on the fishermen's desperation. It scares him to see them going off to their toil when the sea is so rough. Moira, flat out on a lounger, agrees with him. Ever since the storm began, the fishermen have been avoiding the deeper waters. They're nervous. They say they've never seen anything like it, the island isolated in a ring of clouds, fish fleeing from the nets. And the voices.

"What voices?" asks Uli, surprised.

"Don't you know? The fishermen are talking about voices that come up from the sea as soon as they enter the storm. They're scared to go any further, not for fear of the wind and the rain, but because they're terrified of the voices. First you hear a kind of breath, then a murmur, then clear words, and finally shouts. This as the boats keep moving ahead. And that's not all. Commander Juvêncio, the chief of police, who tried to get across the bridge, tells a similar story."

"He heard voices, too?!" asks Daniel, sceptical.

"He says he did. About three hundred metres in, after the bridge has sunk into the mist and it's started to rain. From there onwards, a clamour begins, people talking in different languages. You guys don't know Juvêncio. He's a huge man, brave, who used to be a soldier and bore witness to the worst horrors during the war. Even so, he didn't have the nerve to go on, or to lean out over the waters. He ran back to the island."

Daniel finds legends, beliefs, superstitions and popular fable-making annoying. According to him, the whole process of bewitching the everyday, perpetrated not only by country-folk and rural fishermen, but also by a lot of school-educated people in the big cities, such as Maputo or Luanda, is ruining the credibility of modern African fiction.

"One guy writes about reality and immediately he gets accused of practising outdated magic realism."

"All reality is magic," says Uli. "Quantum physics says that. I'm always thinking about that cat that was alive and dead at the same time. Or about time, that slows while I'm running. Isn't all that magic realism?"

Daniel remembers Jude again. He finds that strange, too, encountering the Nigerian writer, in the middle of the night, chatting telepathically with Baltazar.

"What's more, Luzia says that he was hassling her . . ."

"That's not what Luzia says," Uli corrects him. "She says Jude was impertinent."

"I talked to Jude," adds Moira. "He swore to me that at that time he was in his room, reading one of Uli's books.

He said he was going to find Luzia to straighten things out."

Daniel goes into the pool. He swims three strokes and comes back to the others.

"Hey – that actor, what's his name?"

"Gito?!" Moira doesn't bother to hide her outrage. "You're telling me Gito Bitonga is going around impersonating Jude?"

"I'm not saying anything for sure. I only know that Gito is able to get himself mistaken for Jude. He could have impersonated him just as a joke. Or he puts himself in Jude's skin to get the attention of some girls."

"Don't be idiotic. Anyway, Gito's gay."

"He's gay?!"

"He's the president of Amar, an association that fights for the rights of gay people in the Muslim community."

"He's a Muslim?" asks Uli.

"No, but his husband is."

Daniel gets out of the water and lies down on his back on the deck. The sky is clear – though the horizon remains black, cut through occasionally by the sharp flash of the lightning – and it glows like a large sheet of shocking-blue wax paper. The writer closes his eyes. He sees, sailing across his retina, miniscule pink figures. He thinks he'd like to die like this, in a thousand years' time, in three thousand years' time, exhausted from everything, stretched out beneath the generous African sky.

He is awoken by the voice of Luzia, who has run over to them, very excited.

"You guys aren't going to believe it! That old man, you remember the old Angolan? He's Pedro Calunga Nzagi!"

Daniel gets up, followed by Moira and Uli. They surround the young woman with questions:

"Why do you say that?"

"I talked to him."

"And did the old man admit it?"

"No, he didn't. I realised it was him. He has the same interests."

"The same interests? What do you mean?"

"We got to talking. Suddenly, I thought all the pieces fit."

"Sometimes we see what we want to see," says Daniel. "He's a pleasant chap. It's nice liking him."

"It's him!" Luzia sits down on the deck, turned towards the sea. "I'm sure it's him."

Uli sits down next to her. He gives her his hand.

"You all know, I never knew my father. He left, disappeared when I was three. He was a German doctor. My mother thought the guy went back to Germany. Once, in Berlin, I followed an old man, very respectable-looking, for an entire morning, believing he could be my father. If it weren't for Nzagi, I wouldn't exist as a writer. Or rather, I just wouldn't exist, because, after all, a writer is what I am. I started to write because of him. I would like to meet him, too. But I think Daniel's correct. We see what we want to see."

5

The light from the Indian Ocean is filling the room. Sitting on the bed, Luzia thinks that, if the tide came up just a little higher, the water would soon be right here, gleaming on her feet. She'd like to go out for a run, maybe a swim, but first she has to choose the poems she's going to read the following day. Two years ago, she published a verse novel, entitled *Dona Epifânia Doesn't Want to Marry*, about a woman taxi driver, the Dona Epifânia of the title, who travels from Luanda to the city of Huambo, on Angola's central plateau, to deliver a new-born baby to his father. They have asked her to choose some lines from that novel. On rereading it, she finds some small typos that bother her. She published her first poetry collection at twenty-one. Then another three, plus the novel. One might assume that she had resigned herself to the inevitability of mistakes, which neither she nor the proofreaders had managed to identify and correct. But that's not the case. As she gets older, she gets ever more demanding of herself and of others; less tolerant of her own failings and other people's. "I'll end up a very old lady at thirty-five," she murmurs, because, to her, getting old means coming to resemble her father, a man her best friend Irene once described as "a machine with a stone for a heart".

There is a knock. Luzia gets up, puts on the hotel bathrobe and opens the door. In front of her stands Jude, who suddenly seems shorter ("too little for such an important writer" is what occurs to her) and visibly self-conscious.

"Desculpa," he apologises to her, in Portuguese. "Disseram-me que estás zangado comigo."

The young woman is surprised to hear him speaking Portuguese. Seeing him there, so tiny, so flustered, struggling to communicate in her language, moves her. She wants to invite him in, but she hesitates.

"No, I'm not angry with you. It was strange, that night."

"That wasn't me." He is speaking English now, and his voice is firm.

99

"Oh," thinks Luzia, "now he's going to tell me he'd been drinking." Kiami used to do that, yelling at her in public, almost always out of jealousy, then calling the next morning to apologise: "It wasn't me. It was the wine talking."

"What do you mean 'that wasn't me'?"

"It wasn't me. At that time I was in my room, at the Terraço das Quitandas, reading."

Luzia makes a decision.

"Do you want to get some tea? The restaurant's right by the deck. Wait for me there. I'll be down in five minutes."

Jude agrees. Luzia shuts the door, takes off the robe, puts on a yellow bikini that enhances the black gleam of her skin, ties a kapulana around her chest, arranges her little braids and goes to meet the Nigerian. He is waiting for her, sitting less than a metre from the water. He gets up when he sees her arriving.

"Very beautiful, that kapulana."

Luzia agrees. It was Moira who had given her the kapulana, in the colours of the Angolan flag, red, black and yellow, telling her she'd bought it from the grandchildren of an old lady who had fallen into misfortune but who had been rich and powerful in colonial times. After the grandmother died, the grandchildren found five trunks filled with old kapulanas, a symbol of the deceased woman's status. Jude listens attentively as the young poet talks. He shows her a series of pictures of kapulanas he's taken in recent days, and asks permission to photograph hers. Luzia removes the fabric and lays it out on the table. Jude takes several photos, carefully averting his eyes from her body. The woman is amused by this delicacy of his, this almost shyness, which has nothing in common with the previous night's scene.

"I believe it," she says.

Jude puts the camera down on the table and looks up at her. "You believe me."

"I do. But if it wasn't you, who was that guy?"

"Did he really look that much like me?"

"I don't know anymore. It was pretty dark. Now I think about it, he might have been taller than you."

"Almost all men are taller than me."

("Shit!" thinks Luzia. "What did I say?")

"No, no. You're a normal height."

Jude smiles, amused at her distress. He tells her he spent years wearing shoes with platform soles. He had them custom-made, at an old cobbler's in Lagos, who managed very skilfully to disguise their height. Whenever conference organisers asked him if he preferred to speak standing up, at a lectern, or sitting down, he always went for the second option. He also preferred being photographed sitting down. It took him years to get over his complex.

"You're really not as short as all that," says Luzia. "I'm serious."

"You're right. I've met at least a couple of dwarfs who were shorter than me."

Luzia laughs. She hits him lightly on the shoulder.

"I think I'm the one who ought to be apologising. I should have realised right away it wasn't you."

"That other man, did you call him by my name?"

"I don't remember. I don't think so."

"It couldn't have been that actor, Bitonga?"

Luzia turns serious. The possibility hadn't occurred to her.

"Maybe. The two of you don't look alike, but it's true,

he's very good at imitating your way of speaking, your accent, even your posture. Yeah, it could have been him."

"Either that or *I'm* Bitonga. And the other one, the one who was hassling you, he really was Jude D'Souza."

They both laugh. However, back in her bedroom, lying on her bed, Luzia thinks about the joke and no longer finds it so funny. She looks for Jude's novel, the Portuguese edition, which she bought months ago, on a visit to Lisbon. On the inside cover there's a photo of him. He's sitting on a chair, his face resting on his right fist, and looking into the camera, serene and focused as a chess grandmaster. The woman opens the book and starts to read. As she reads, the afternoon is erased, bit by bit.

6

Daniel and Uli are in the yard, sitting in the shade of the big lemon tree, drinking iced tea and talking about the strange storm that's settled on to the mainland, the voices coming from the sea, how terribly they're missing the internet, when Moira comes in, holding on to her belly – sweaty and breathless. The Angolan jumps to his feet.

"Have your waters broken?"

Moira sits down on a charpai. She flaps at the air with a fan while struggling to recover her breath.

"What do you mean, my waters?! I've already told you, the baby won't be arriving now."

"What, then?"

"Come with me."

"Where?"

"To the police station."

"The police station? What for?"

Moira had been at the Santo António church, working, when a policeman appeared with a message from Commander Juvêncio. A woman had come over the bridge on foot. The guards had found it strange, because since the storm began, nobody had got on or off the island, so they detained her and went to call the police. The woman seemed drugged or drunk, talking a language nobody could understand. Maybe she was – the commander had thought – a guest of the festival's.

"Are you expecting another woman writer?" asks Uli.

"Yes," says Moira. "A novelist from Senegal, Fatou Diome. And there are two men who've disappeared, too – Breytenbach and Gonçalo Tavares."

"Could be the Senegalese woman," says Daniel, "but how did she get here on her own?"

7

There are two boys. One of them is carrying a huge fish on his head. The other holds out his hand, pointing at something outside the frame of the photograph, and, with this gesture, his arm cuts in front of the face of the first. Ofélia, sitting on a long bench, in the main hall of the Hotel Villa Sands art gallery, studies the image. "There's something we can't see," she thinks, "just as we can't see the first boy's eyes." What appeals to her in the photo is not what it shows, but what it hides:

1) Whatever the boy is pointing at.
2) The blind gaze of the other boy.

Luzia sits down next to her.

"I was sure I'd find you here," she says.

Ofélia hadn't sensed her arrival. She looks at her with a flicker of annoyance, because she hates being interrupted when she is alone, lost to her thoughts and daydreams. But as soon as her eyes light on the other woman, she understands that something's wrong. She hugs her.

"What's happened, child?"

"I'm scared."

"Why?"

Luzia points behind her, towards the door. If the two women turned their heads (they do not), they would see the fish market and, beyond it, the rusty carcass of a ship tossed onto the beach. In the distance, the dark horizon.

"The storm?" Ofélia asks.

"Yeah, the storm. And also myself, my own private storms. Sometimes I'm scared I'm not even real."

"You aren't," Ofélia assures her, impassive. "You only exist while I'm thinking about you."

"Solipsism."

"You see? It was me who put that word into your mouth."

"Seriously now. Don't you sense there's something wrong?"

"Almost everything."

"I mean, on this island."

"You're only feeling that because of the internet. Or rather, because we have no internet."

"What do you mean?"

"You've been suffering withdrawal from virtual reality for days now. Actually, that expression, 'virtual reality', it's a strange one . . ."

"Oh, I know, a contradiction in terms."

"We spend more and more time sunk into that unreal reality. When we're deprived of it, we find the experience weird. Something similar happens if we spend ten hours in a row reading a good novel. The moment we finally put the book down and stand up, the world around us feels fake, incoherent, not altogether solid. Isn't that what it's like? But that wasn't why you came looking for me."

"It wasn't?"

"I don't think so. When a woman seeks out another woman, and she's got those sleepy eyes and that beautiful little shocked expression, there's always a man on the horizon."

"Nonsense. There's no man."

"Jude, I'm guessing."

"He came to see me."

"To your room?"

"Yeah."

"And? Did you end up in bed?"

"No, no! We went for tea."

"I don't know what's with you, girl. I swear! When I was your age, divine little bod like that, I never would have let him get away."

"I'm starting to understand why you write about sex so much."

"There's no other subject."

"There are plenty of other subjects."

"No. What you think are other subjects are merely derivations from the one primordial proposition. Or alternatively escapes. And I've never been one to run away. Did you know I was in the Maquis?"

"Yes, everyone knows that."

"And do you know what my nom de guerre was?"

"No."

"Ngueve, it's hippopotamus in Umbundo. Not just because I had a twin sister, that old tradition, but because I enjoy a good fight and because when I bite, I bite to kill. Now tell me: what is it about the lad that scares you."

"I don't know who he is. I can't figure it out."

"Excellent. Run a mile from the predictable ones. Have you read the book?"

"I'm reading it now. I think it's very good."

"Does that get you excited?"

"Excuse me?!"

"His intelligence."

"I guess so."

"Sex, girl. Sex is the answer. Take him to bed as soon as you can. You'll see, you'll feel better, more fully realised, and more real."

8

The woman is wearing a blue boubou. Her head – crowned in a huge turban, in different shades of the same colour – is balancing with some difficulty on a long and very narrow neck. She paces from side to side of the police chief's small office, never resting her eyes on anybody.

"Do you know who she is?" asks Juvêncio.

Moira has never seen a picture of Fatou Diome. She can't confirm it's her. She positions herself in front of the woman.

"Fatou? Fatou Diome?"

The woman doesn't reply. She starts pacing even faster, almost bumping into the walls, while at the same time waving her thin arms, randomly hurling out sharp and mysterious words. Moira speaks to her in French, then in English. Nothing.

"She comes from the other coast," says Daniel. "Yes, she could be Senegalese. But also Nigerian or Malian."

"The people are unsettled," says Juvêncio, stroking his enormous belly. "They think she's a bloodsucker."

Daniel looks at him, astonished.

"A bloodsucker?"

"A night creature," Uli explains. "Ancestral spirits that attack people in the darkness. They drink their blood. In short, vampires."

"And nobody else crossed the bridge?" asks Moira. "She was alone?"

Juvêncio confirms this. The woman crossed on foot, at the head of a flock of crows, emerging from the storm with her clothes dry and her tall turban neatly arranged on her head, like a luminous slice she had stolen from the island's clear sky. Uli tells them that right there, in Muhipiti, a good twenty years ago, he too had been mistaken for a bloodsucker. He arrived in the company of a team of five biologists, three of them English, at a time when the population was going through some terrible troubles. The rumour that there was a bloodsucker in the group spread fast, fuelled by the recent passing of two children, who had died of cholera. The then chief of police, a thin, fearful chap by the name of Malan, advised them to quit the island before spirits got even more agitated. They put all their luggage into two cars and off they went, with Malan taking the lead, pedalling a decrepit bicycle. At the exit from the bridge there was a small crowd armed with katanas, sticks and stones. "There's nothing I can do," said Malan regretfully, pedalling hurriedly away. Uli got out of the car and faced the mob: "What's the problem?" One old man, with a katana in each hand, took two timid steps forward: "They say you're bloodsuckers." Uli took a deep breath. He shouted: "Yes, we're bloodsuckers, all of us!" The human mass trembled. One woman burst into distressed screams. Another started to cry. Uli shouted again: "We're bloodsuckers, but we don't mean to stay here any longer. The blood of Makuas is no good at all, it tastes of piss. The blood of the Machangana, oh yeah, man, that's nice and sweet. So good. Let us out and we will never return."

Juvêncio followed the story with an amused smile.

"And they did get out, of course, or the writer wouldn't be here today."

"They moved aside and we left," Uli concludes. "The bigger problem was the smell, because one of the Englishmen was so scared he crapped himself."

The group's laughter disturbs the woman. For the first time, she seems to notice that she is not alone. She looks with amazement at Daniel, pressing her nose right up to his face, as though smelling him, shaking her head, moaning and cracking her knuckles. Finally she squats down in one corner of the room, very still, with her eyes shut. The Angolan writer sits down, distressed.

"What the hell was that?"

Moira kisses his forehead.

"Take it easy, love. This woman isn't well."

Juvêncio scratches his scalp.

"I don't know what to do with her. I can't let her go in that state, besides which, she hasn't got any papers. Seems like she's a foreign citizen here irregularly."

"And there's also that rumour about her," says Uli. "Best to keep her here. There's no doctor who could see her?"

"We've only got one doctor on the island, but he went on a trip last week."

"She needs seeing by a psychiatrist," says Moira. "There's no psychiatrist on the island. Maybe in Nampula or Nacala. We've got to wait for the storm to pass."

9

Júlio Zivane does not like drinking alone, shut up at home or in a hotel room. He prefers to get drunk in open spaces, surrounded by strangers, who won't try to talk him out of it, feeling neither pity nor revulsion towards him, and who at most would say, as young Ezequiel does, at this moment: "Old man, maybe it'd be better for you to head back to your hotel, take a shower and sleep it off."

Ezequiel isn't the owner of the Afamado bar – an establishment that, though its name rather pretentiously means "renowned", is really just a small wooden hut with a green-painted counter, behind which the lad is huddled, sweating heavily, as he passes out more or less cold beers and soft drinks. Ezequiel knew that Júlio was an incomer – as all visitors are called on the island – the moment he saw him appear in the distance, stopping, astonished, beside the high walls of the fortress. His uncle had told him not to bother the customers with questions. This lad, however, is curious, and he can't resist:

"Maputo?" he asked, handing over the first of many beers Zivane would drink that night.

The writer glanced at him with some impatience.

"I've come from very far away."

He was from Maputo, definitely, judging not by his accent but by his attitude. Ezequiel didn't ask him anything else. He watched him move away, the beer in one hand and a book in the other, and sit down on one of the garden benches. He drank that first bottle greedily. The rest of them, slowly, enjoying the cool night-time breeze. Each time he returned to the bar, in search of another beer, Zivane came more slowly, weaving hesitant little steps in the sand, as if the air were gaining in thickness as the light drained away.

"He's already taking longer to get here than to swallow his beer," thinks Ezequiel. Calmly, without raising his voice, he suggests that the writer go back to his hotel. The man puts his book and the bottle down on the bar, leans on his elbows, shuts his eyes and stays silent for a long while, as if Ezequiel's comment demands serious and careful consideration.

"You're quite right," he says at last. "Have a good night."

He turns his back and moves away. He is just getting ready to cross the garden, which looks, at that time, bigger and darker than the night itself, when he notices a squalid old man, straight-backed, sitting on the same bench where he has been drinking. Zivane rubs his eyes, with an expression that mixes incredulity and terror.

"Fuck, I've had too much to drink!"

The old man looks up, throwing him a glance that is filled with reproach.

"Ah, senhor, you disappoint me," he says, patting the bench. "Sit!"

Júlio Zivane sits as far as he can from the old man. He looks down, unable to face him.

"It's not possible . . ."

"You are not ashamed?"

The writer tries to get up; however, the old man grabs him by the arm, tenacious and strong.

"Sit, I told you!"

"What do you want from me?"

"Dignity! Have a bit of dignity, for the love of God! Do not stain the good name of our ancestors."

Zivane feels like he's falling, the way stars fall into black holes, with their light getting sucked in first, and then matter and then time. He yanks his arm free, gets up, and runs, tripping on the roots of the century-old banyans, crying, moaning, while the past with shrieks pursues him.

Ezequiel watches him disappearing into the night. He shakes his head, with a mocking smile: "Drunks!" And only then does he notice the book that the incomer forgot on the small counter. He picks it up. The title intrigues him: *Dona Epifânia Doesn't Want to Marry*, by Luzia Valente. He sits down and starts to read.

10

Daniel is dreaming about Baltazar. The tramp is sitting on the sand of the beach, with a small blackwood strongbox at his feet. He opens the box and pulls out a handful of transparent little stones. "What are they?", Daniel wants to know. The other man opens his lips, which are painted dark blue, in a wicked smile: "Time crystals. Swallow them. You'll see the centuries as if they were days. The millennia dancing around you, and all of it distinctly, every moment quite still, looking at you as if in a photograph." With these words, he puts one of the stones in Daniel's mouth. "Swallow it!", he commands.

"What was it, my love?" Moira looks at him, worried. "You were crying."

Daniel remembers Baltazar and the time crystals. However, no sooner has he started to recount the dream, than it comes apart, like a ruined palace in the desert, so that the Angolan can remember nothing of what happened after he swallowed the crystal, not one image, not one line of dialogue. All that remains is a vast sorrow, which takes his breath away, squeezing his chest.

"I'm just feeling so anxious," he admits to his wife. "I don't know why."

"Must be because of the birth."

"It's not, truly, I'm not at all worried about the birth. It's all going to go fine."

He is worried. However, he thinks it would be useless and even cruel to expose her to his fears. He tries to control his anxieties, telling himself that babies are born every day in more difficult conditions, and in most cases, they land happy in our world. Besides, the anxiety tormenting him is not connected to the birth. It comes from somewhere else, some place darker and deeper.

THE FOURTH DAY

Reality is an accidental by-product of fiction.

ULÍ LIMA LEVY, interviewed by the newspaper *El País*, on
29 February 2019, a few days before the beginning of the end.

I

Luzia wakes up on her side, with the sensation that there's somebody stretched out, motionless, behind her. This happens often, and yet it always scares her. It's a few minutes past one in the morning. The young woman gets up, opens the door leading to the veranda, and goes out. The hot, humid air sticks to her body like a silk dressing-gown. There is a man sitting on the deck, facing out to sea – but there is no sea. The water looks like it's retreated almost to the horizon. The silhouettes of the boats buried in the sand rise up to meet the Milky Way. The girl thinks she could live on that island forever. She imagines herself for a moment getting old at one of the tables of the Âncora d'Ouro café, watching the boys outside turning into old men, and then she decides, no, best to stay in Luanda, absorbing the big city's noisy energy, sometimes crying, almost always laughing, even when everything seems lost.

She puts on a short, light dress, printed with strelitzia flowers, then leaves the room and walks down to the deck, certain that she has recognised the man who is sitting there, watching the horizon.

"Is it you?"

Jude turns to her, smiling.

"Who?"

"Jude D'Souza. The real thing."

"I don't know. How can I know?"

"What are you doing here?"

"I couldn't sleep. I walked over from my hotel, along the sand. The tide's low."

Luzia sits down next to him.

"I need to be sure it's really you. What did we talk about this afternoon?"

"Yesterday afternoon. Last time I looked at my watch, it was already gone midnight."

"Right. Yesterday afternoon."

"I confessed my best-kept secret to you . . ."

"Your secret? What secret?"

"I'm a dwarf."

Luzia laughs. She wants to hug him. But she's worried she might frighten him. After all, Jude's practically English and she knows that Europeans, with the exception of Italians in the south, find more exuberant displays of affection weird. She points at a patch of sky that is totally dark.

"I don't know anything about astronomy, but I noticed the other night that there isn't a single star there. Don't you think that's weird?"

Jude's eyes plunge into that precise darkness. He has been watching the night for more than half an hour and hasn't managed to see it. He's had no practice looking at stars.

"You're right," he says. "It's as if there is some big solid object in space, blocking out the light."

"I'm sorry I never studied astronomy. We're like two

illiterates in a library. We've got this open book right in front of us and we can't read it."

"I can make something up if you like."

"Go ahead."

"That constellation there. See it? The one that looks like the head of a crowned crane? Or alternatively a strelitzia? It's called 'The Poetess'."

"Seriously? Why?"

"I'll tell you the story. Once upon a time there was a poetess who likes strelitzias. She wanted to be able to speak the language of plants, but she was lacking organs in her body to do that. She was lacking senses. And so she decided to bury herself in the ground up to the neck, in the hope that, that way, she might get roots."

"And did she?"

"No. She got a fungal infection. Then she decided to lie in the sun, in the hope that, by doing this, she might get leaves."

"And did she?"

"No. She got a terrible sunburn. However, Zeus was moved by her determination, he transformed her into a strelitzia and placed her in the middle of the sky."

"I liked it. How did you guess?"

"Guess what?"

"That I wish I could talk to plants."

"I didn't guess. I read your first book, *Playing with Firearms*."

"That's true – how embarrassing!"

"Why embarrassing?"

"I write without knowing what I write. I don't reread my books once they've been published. Later, when I hear readers commenting on them, I realise I've exposed too much of myself. I'm much more naked in my books than when I take off my clothes."

There's an amused laugh behind them, immediately followed by an unmistakable voice.

"Aren't we all. A library is a nudist beach."

The two writers turn around, like synchronised swimmers, with an identical expression of surprise and shock. Uli is lying on one of the loungers, next to the pool, wearing only a pair of Bermudas, his hair tousled, his blue eyes shining behind their small round glasses. Luzia gets up and goes over to him.

"I didn't see you."

Uli stands up, and greets her with a kiss on each cheek. He apologises. He'd left his room to get a bit of fresh air, lain down on a lounger, looking at the sea, and fallen asleep. He woke up to the sound of their voices, just in time to hear Luzia admit that she feels naked every time she publishes a new book.

"That was all you heard?" asks Luzia, doubtful.

"Did I miss something important?"

"You missed the story of a constellation," says Jude.

"You've got a good title there for your next novel: *The Story of a Constellation.* I'm very sorry. I didn't mean to disturb you. Truly. I'll go back to my official bed."

"Stay," says Luzia. "I suggest we play a game."

"What game?" Uli asks.

"I'll call it 'The Game of Fiction and Reality'. Each of us tells two short stories. One true, the other made up. The others need to guess which is the true one, which the invented one. Who'll go first?"

"You start," says Uli. "It was your idea."

"Fine. First story. When I was fifteen, they caught an intruder in our house. My brother woke me up. The guards had found a man in the yard. They stripped him and tied him to a chair, in the garage, with a piece of nylon cord, those ones people use as a laundry line. He was a thin little man, with a long face and small scared eyes that never stayed still. I remember seeing my father standing in front of him, a paddle in his hand. 'Have you come here to steal?' The man said no and my father hit him hard on one leg. He asked the question again. The man said he was a quimbandeiro and that he'd been flying over the city when, suddenly, he didn't feel well and he fell. They tortured him till the small hours of the morning, but the man stuck to his story. Finally, they let him go."

"Is that how it ends?" asks Uli.

"No. They let him go because he aged during the course of the night. He aged before their eyes. They were worried he'd die of old age."

"I liked it," said Jude. "Let's have the second."

"The second story happened a little later. At seventeen, I fell in love with my maths teacher. My best friend, Ruth, who was secretly dating the PE teacher, this really handsome young Cuban guy, was appalled. The maths teacher was over forty, he had a stutter and he wore white shirts, tucked into his trousers. He had a beautiful voice and he spoke with passion, not just about maths but also about music, cinema, literature and politics. He had been imprisoned for several years, before I was even born, and he was connected to a small opposition party. I started sending him messages by email. First, made-up questions about maths, then true existential questions and love poems. Roberto, he was called Roberto, replied to all the questions and ignored the poems. One day I went into his office, tore off my blouse and skirt and pressed him up against the wall. Unfortunately the headmistress opened the door and caught us. The teacher was fired. My father threatened to kill him, and poor Roberto was forced to run away to Portugal. He came back, many years later, and married Ruth. They have two children."

"Both stories are true," says Uli. "But the first is truer than the second . . ."

"No, no!" Luzia interrupts him. "It's only at the end, when we've all told our stories, that you can say what you think."

"OK," Uli agrees. "Let's hear Jude now."

Jude describes how, when he was in Lisbon, gathering elements for his novel, he was introduced to a former officer in the Portuguese army, the son, grandson and great-grandson of soldiers who had fought in Africa. This man invited him to dinner at his house, a large decaying villa on the outskirts of Lisbon, where he kept his impressive collection of old guns, trophies of war, maps and books about the former colonies. They dined alone, a melancholy hake accompanied by three boiled potatoes, all served on silver tableware bearing the distinguished family's crest. After dessert – a banana apiece – the officer invited him to visit the library. Then he showed him, with great pride, a glass jar with the head, preserved in formaldehyde, of an African king.

Uli whistles.

"You're lying!"

"Fiction or reality, you'll decide that at the end," Luzia scolds him. "Tell your second story, Jude."

"Right. The other story happened in Lagos. My paternal

grandmother was a remarkable woman, a warrior who raised twelve children on her own. One night, she must have been around seventy, she drank more than usual. She woke the next morning with terrible pains in her right leg. She opened her eyes to see a huge boa constrictor, which had swallowed her entire leg all the way to the groin. It couldn't progress any further, but nor could it retreat, because the curved fangs, gripping onto the flesh, wouldn't allow that, so there it was, struggling, every bit as desperate as my grandmother. The yells woke the whole village. One of my uncles appeared, with a katana, and cut the boa into pieces. The skin on my grandmother's leg was in a very bad way and never went back to its original colour. She came to be known as 'the white-legged woman'."

Luzia sits down on the deck, holding her belly, helpless with pure and contagious laughter. Uli shakes his head, defeated.

"This guy is the king of the liars," he said in Portuguese. "I don't stand a chance."

Jude looks at them both, amused.

"Uli's turn. I want to hear."

"No," says Uli. "It's not worth it."

"Go on," says Luzia. "You're going to make Mozambique look bad otherwise."

The Mozambican writer concedes. He sits down next to Luzia. The girl nestles in his arms. Uli recounts how, fifteen years earlier, that same island had gone through some turbulent days after a devout Muslim fisherman, Abdul Abdala Suleimane, better known at the time as Dulinho and today as Flyer, announced his intention to make a pilgrimage to Mecca via the sky, doing without aeroplanes, helicopters, balloons, dirigibles or any other means of air transportation devised by man. At first they teased him. That didn't bother him. What differentiates a simple lunatic from a visionary is his determination. The fisherman was so insistent about his plan, which would require only a good launch pad pointed in the direction of Mecca, that eventually people stopped laughing at him and began to offer him support. The president of the local council secured the necessary funds for the construction of the runway, with two or three donors supplying a little money for putting up the stands. On the morning of the launch, the city awoke all decked out for a celebration. The people filled the streets in a great festive euphoria. What began as a day of pride – soon an islander was going to be known the world over as the first person to fly, like a bird, to Mecca – ended in shame and disappointment. Dulinho, dressed in a beautiful white kaftan, and holding two yellow parasols, one in each hand, tried to rise up into the air, once, twice, three times, but you couldn't say that he flew, that would be an exaggeration, he merely flapped about clumsily, like a chicken, rising only to the height of the stands, only then quickly to crash-land, rolling ingloriously along the runway. The crowd who moments earlier had been cheering him on, now turned against him. The council president himself led by example, grabbing a stone from the pavement and hurling it with all his strength at the poor wretch's head. That first stone did not hit its target, but several others did, so that Dulinho ended up in a hospital bed, very badly beaten.

Luzia claps.

"Great! Terrific story. Let's have the next."

"Yes!" says Jude. "Tell us another."

"I'm going to tell you about something that happened to me. I've always been interested in all the traditional forms of fortune-telling. I learned to throw the tinhlolo from an old Nguni medicine-woman I met years ago and whom I still see pretty often. One day, travelling round Germany to promote the translation of one of my novels, I made the stupid mistake of revealing this interest, and I even showed my tools, my little bones and shells, which I happened to have with me in my rucksack. This was at a literary festival, in Berlin. There were a lot of other authors around. Not many people at my event. Nevertheless, when they set me up at a little table for the customary signings, I realised that the line was very much longer than I could have predicted, and it was still growing. Most people were not there for me to sign their books. What they did intend was a consultation. With the help of my translator, Herbert Borchmeyer, we divided the people up into two lines, those who had come for a signing, whom I dispatched in ten minutes, and the rest. I spent three hours on these others and I didn't deal with even a third of them. There was a bit of everything. People who wanted to know the future. Poor wretches with incurable illnesses. Women suffering from impossible loves. Back at the hotel, my translator asked me if the spirits might help him track down an old girlfriend, who'd disappeared seven years earlier and whom he'd never heard from again. 'A consultation like this only allows me to say why this or that happened, or to prepare the consulter for what might happen next,' I explained. We sat down and I cast the shells. The girlfriend was somewhere very nearby. She would show up soon. My friend laughed, not believing me. That night, while we were having dinner at the hotel restaurant, a woman approached us. She stood there, wordless, staring at Herbert, who went pale, standing up slowly. They hugged awkwardly, like two strangers at a funeral, and then they went off, leaving me to dine alone. I didn't see Herbert again till the next afternoon, in the hotel lobby, while I was waiting for the taxi that would take us to the airport. I didn't dare ask what had happened."

Uli falls silent. Luzia and Jude look at each other, disconcerted.

"That's how your story ends?" asks Luzia.

"It is. To this day Herbert has never told me what happened with that girlfriend. Why she disappeared, and why she reappeared again so many years later, all of a sudden, right in front of us."

"If your story was true, that would make sense," said Jude. "Life rarely offers us solutions. But you also could have invented a malformed ending just so that your story would *seem* more true."

"Could be," Uli agrees. "So, what do you both bet?"

"I think Luzia's first story is genuine and the second she made up," says Jude. "Uli's are both true."

"I also think Uli's are both true," says Luzia. "As are yours. You've both cheated. We agreed that one story would be true and the other would be made up."

"You're right," Uli concedes. "We did cheat, me and Jude. But unlike him, I reckon you did, too. I think both your stories are equally true."

"Seriously?!" Jude is surprised.

Luzia bursts out laughing.

"You got me. It all happened."

When he finally returns to his room, Uli Lima will think there's nothing like life for spinning good stories. He lies on his bed and waits for sleep to come. It doesn't. Then he goes over to sit at the desk, opens his laptop and starts to write.

2

It was Moira who had the idea of driving the undocumented woman to the Terraço das Quitandas, in the hope that the Nigerian writers might be able to communicate with her. Commander Juvêncio accompanied the two women, curious to learn the outcome of a case that had been troubling the populace. He had gone to bed late, having spent hours resolving minor conflicts, all resulting from rumours that had been circulating since the storm began. Two days earlier, after lunch, he had decided to cross the bridge himself on foot, ahead of a small group of police officers and citizens, to prove that the world was continuing as normal on the other side. Or rather, to prove that the world on the other side was still there at all. "The world has ended. Only the island is left," many people were saying, offering as evidence for the disaster the fact that they were deprived of news from the rest of the country and the planet. They managed the first five hundred metres without any trouble. But as soon as they entered the rain, his officers' morale began to weaken. "Boss," said his right-hand man, a sergeant as calm as an ox, called Ali Habib, "best we go back. The wind's blowing too strong. We're all going to fly away, like Abdul Abdala Suleimane."

Juvêncio reminded him that the Flyer had never actually flown, not even to Ilha de Goa, let alone to Mecca, and as they recalled that historical failure, they progressed a few metres further. "Boss, can't you hear the voices?" asked Ali Habib, who was seconded in this by the other men. The commander could hear nothing but the loud howl of the wind, the raging of the sea, the harsh roar of the rain beating the asphalt. He leaned out over the handrail. He saw the ferocious waves, the foam flying, the sky fighting against the water. When he turned around again, his men were no longer there. The fog was so thick that, for a few moments, he couldn't tell if he was moving forward or back. And thus, he let the gale return him to the island.

The woman walks between Moira and the commander, without resisting, but also without showing any curiosity or concern about where she is being taken. They go into the hotel, up the stairs, through corridors and across long halls lavishly decorated with pieces of African art, till they come to one of the verandas, where they find Cornelia and Jude, who are drinking tea and talking.

"I figured you'd be here," says Moira. "We need your help."

She introduces them to Commander Juvêncio. She explains that the woman was found on the bridge, without papers, and that it was generally agreed that she'd come from the mainland. She didn't speak Makua, or Portuguese, or French or English. They presumed from her dress that she came originally from West Africa.

"Yes," Cornelia confirms this, intrigued. "She looks Nigerian."

She addresses a few words to the woman. The woman

emerges from her apathy, answering the writer's questions with brusque words, without even looking straight at her, spinning around, rubbing her hands and twisting her head. Jude also asks her some questions. The conversation continues for several long minutes, getting ever more intense, until, all of a sudden, Cornelia gets up, says something to Jude, and runs off to her room in tears.

"What happened?" asks Moira.

Jude gets up and starts clapping, though there is more mockery in his gesture than admiration.

"Congratulations. You guys have done great work. And what a remarkable actress! Cornelia was caught totally off guard, she's been really on edge lately. Maybe it'd be best if I go try to calm her down . . ."

"What are you saying?" Moira gets annoyed. "What actress?"

Then the woman runs off, very fast, along the hallway and down the stairs, followed by the commander, who's shouting "Get her! Get her!" but it quickly becomes clear that nobody's going to get her, least of all Juvêncio. Moira and Jude go over to the guardrail, in time to see the Nigerian woman leaving the hotel, at great speed, and disappearing around the nearest corner.

"She's not an actress?!" Jude is astonished.

"What do you mean, actress? I don't know who she is! What did you three talk about?"

"Seriously, she isn't an actress?" Jude sits down. He fills a glass of water and drinks. "I thought she was an actress."

Juvêncio returns breathless, sweating heavily.

"Did you see how she ran?"

Moira sits down next to Jude, holding her belly. She feels like it's about to burst, the way the dams burst from the water pressure after the heavy rains. Juvêncio sees how distressed she is and kneels beside her.

"Calm down now. Take deep breaths."

"I don't want to take deep breaths. I want to know what happened." She turns to Jude. "Who the hell is she?"

"The cockroach," says Jude. "She's the cockroach-woman."

3

They are in the Âncora d'Ouro café. They have pushed two tables together so that everyone can fit. Daniel, sitting beside Moira, has his arm around her waist, while she describes what happened at the Terraço das Quitandas. Uli Lima laughs out loud. He shuts up, however, when he looks at his friend's face and sees how afraid she is.

"Oh, come on, kid! It's a joke."

"If it's a joke, I don't find it remotely funny," says Moira. "I really don't find it funny at all."

"I think it's a joke too," Jude butts in. "And unlike Moira, I think it's a very amusing one, very well executed. Unfortunately, it's come at the wrong time. People are on edge because of the storm. This business of having no phones or internet is starting to make us all crazy."

"Have you talked to Cornelia?" asks Moira.

"I have."

"And?"

"You saw the way she reacted. It really disturbed her."

"What did the woman say to the two of you?"

"For me, it was like we were acting in a scene opposite Cornelia's character. I was enjoying myself. For Cornelia, who's been so anxious lately, it must have been like penetrating the darkest spaces of her own mind. She couldn't handle it. Cornelia thinks she's in hell. That's what she said to me: 'We're all dead, brother, we're all in hell.'"

Júlio Zivane, who has thus far kept silent, listening to the other writers while drinking the contents of a litre-and-a-half bottle of mineral water on his own, slaps the table so hard that one of the glasses falls over.

"I saw my father!"

"What are you saying?" asks Uli, appalled. "Your father died more than twenty years ago."

"I saw him. I talked to him. It's true I'd already had a lot to drink, I was terribly drunk, but I saw him," Zivane insists. "None of you gets it. My father is my main character. Luzia here saw Jude's character. Jude saw Cornelia's character . . ."

"You're suggesting our characters are about to occupy the streets?" asks Jude, amused. "I think that's brilliant."

"They're actors," says Daniel, unconvinced. "Some group from Maputo."

Moira disagrees. She knows everyone who makes theatre in Mozambique. She'd know if any group was here. Luzia suggests it might be some international collective. In Amsterdam, three years ago, during a literary festival, she had met a group of Catalan actors who challenged people on the streets, in the skin of famous characters from universal literature: Miss Marple, Lolita, Humbert Humbert, Leopold

Bloom, Lestat, the Three Musketeers, Alice and the Cheshire Cat. Ofélia jumps in to defend Cornelia:

"The woman's right," she says, "we're dead, all totally dead, but the island isn't paradise, or hell, it's purgatory. We'll never get out of this place till we've reconciled with one another, and especially with our ghosts."

"I like that idea," says Zivane. "The best thing about being dead is that I no longer have to die. On the other hand, I don't fancy talking to my father. I've been arguing with him all these years. We've talked, we've got angry, we've made up again countless times. I want to live my death far away from that son of a bitch."

4

Cornelia opens WhatsApp and writes a message to Pierre:

"I'm scared. Come get me. I love you very much."

She taps the blue arrow, to send it, though she knows the message won't go. She only woke up a few hours ago and she's already written more than thirty of these. Hundreds in the last few days. If the internet suddenly starts working again, how will Pierre receive that torrent of words? She imagines the phone beeping non-stop, her husband excusing himself, leaving the classroom at a run (Pierre teaches creative writing). She smiles at that image, then moves from smiling to tears, because that's never going to happen, the internet is never coming back, she's never getting off this island.

The hotel has its own generator. It's been working uninterruptedly the last few days. Unfortunately it's no longer possible to buy fuel on the island, so the manager has opted to turn the device on only between three and seven in the afternoon. The bedroom is an oven. Even with the windows open, it's hard to breathe. Cornelia tried going out onto the huge terrace and quickly drew back again, blinded by the glare. There is only one sun in the sky; yet a thousand more burn tirelessly on the wide whitewashed expanse. Hell is white.

The only bearable place must be the covered veranda, the place where they serve the meals. Cornelia, however, isn't keen to see anybody and she's sure the other guests will this very moment be seeking refuge on the veranda, half-naked, swimming in their own sweat and drinking warm beer.

"Damn those dead people!" she shouts.

She feels sorry for having shouted. One of the dead might have heard her, been offended, and come into her room to ask for explanations, because those morons still haven't grasped their new condition and are exchanging trivialities as if they were alive and unaware of eternal damnation.

She thinks about the cockroach-woman. When she published the book in the United States, every journalist, without exception, asked her about Kafka: what's her relationship to that writer's work? How old was she when she read him first? Is Kafka popular in Nigeria? Cornelia never told them the truth: that the idea for the character hadn't come from a reading of *Metamorphosis*. The cockroach-woman appeared in her life very early. Between the ages of two and six she was raised by an aunt, in a suburban part of Lagos, while her mother, as an immigrant in New York, struggled for survival, studying and working, first as a stripper and then as a fortune-teller, before completing her studies and securing a good job in a bank. Her aunt made a bit of money braiding hair at home. Not having anyone to leave her with, she used to lock her in the kitchen whenever she needed to go out and didn't want to take her along. There was a small window set into the top of the kitchen door, through which, during the day, a meagre light came in. If it got dark before her aunt returned, little Cornelia would watch, terrified, the rapture of the cockroaches. They would burst out in their dozens from the floor and the walls, and very soon they'd fill the small room, greeting one another like fellow guests at a party, while they looked for leftovers of dreams or of food forgotten there by the people. The girl would stay absolutely still, unable to move, feeling the light feet run across her body. One night when her aunt was taking a long time to get back and all her muscles had begun to ache (you try staying totally still for three hours), she heard a very tiny voice, then another, and yet another, and realised, astonished, that she was able to hear the cockroaches' conversation, even if she wasn't able to understand what they were saying. In the years that followed, she didn't just learn to communicate with the insects but became very close to one of them. Such a good friend, in fact, that she began to imagine her as a girl of her age: Lucy, the cockroach-girl.

And now there she is, on an island lost to the world, and the cockroach-girl has grown up and has come to fetch her. But they are no longer friends.

5

Jude takes a seat in the back row. From there he can watch not only the small stage, where Luzia and Ofélia are sitting, but also the rest of the audience. He sees, two rows ahead of him, the old man who'd wanted to know how he imagined the future of Africa. The man has a broad back, solid and straight. His very white hair, cropped short, adds a dignified air to his appearance. He turns – as though in response to Jude's attention – and his lively eyes, animated by a flicker of irony, meet the writer's. They greet each other with a slight nod.

The discussion is being chaired by the Portuguese journalist Pedro Caminha, himself likewise a poet, who lives in Maputo and is very familiar with the literary output of the continent.

"We're going to talk about the traps of identity," says Caminha, straightening his sweaty shirt over his ample belly. "The two poets joining me, Luzia Valente and Ofélia Eastermann, have been working, in their books, though in quite different ways, on questions linked to the formation of an Angolan identity."

"Not me," Ofélia interrupts him. "I write because it turns me on. I get so wet when a good line occurs to me. I couldn't care less about Angolan identity."

The audience laugh. Pedro Caminha smiles amiably. He's used to provocation.

"I always say, books know more than their authors do," he remarks, and now he has the audience laughing with him. Ofélia laughs, too. "Even if Ofélia might not be aware of it, her poetry, having the body and desire as its centre, does support a particular identitarian philosophy. Luzia's supports a different one. What I feel, and I might be wrong, correct me if this isn't the case, is that for you, individual identity is more important than national identity."

"No doubt. I hate being introduced as an Angolan poet. I want to be Ofélia Eastermann, who, among many other aspects, is a poet and Angolan. My identity is limited neither to my nationality nor to being favoured by some possible outbreaks of poetry."

"I don't think very differently," says Luzia. "Only I do think that what I write flows from my being Angolan. I write the way I do because I'm Angolan. I could go further: I write because I'm Angolan."

After the event has finished, Jude remains in his seat, eyes fixed on Luzia, who is talking with a group of students. He doesn't notice when the old man sits down next to him.

"She's very beautiful."

Jude looks at him, with a start.

"Yes. Very beautiful."

"Have you read *Dona Epifânia Doesn't Want to Marry*?"

"I have read it, in Portuguese. I might not have understood it all. My Portuguese is very basic."

The old man gets up. Jude imitates him, feeling even shorter than usual. He looks up and sees the other man's eyes, shining with mockery and (this is how it seems to him) also tenderness. The man holds out his strong, bulky hand and Jude gives him his.

"Treat her well," says the old man, crushing his hand. "We Angolans look out for one another."

Jude goes outside into the light. He feels dizzy and

confused, maybe from the sudden glare and the heat; or could it be from the harsh smell of fish? Before him there rises up the rusty carcass of a ship, like the harbinger of a dream. The writer reels. He sits on the dirty sand of the beach. A boy crouches beside him and opens his palm, showing a handful of old coins corroded by time and by the sea.

"I'll take a thousand meticals," he says. "For the lot."

Jude shuts his eyes. When he opens them again, there is a mirror in front of him. That's what he thinks: "It's a mirror-seller." But there is no mirror-seller. There is no mirror at all. A guy sitting in front of him, who looks identical, throws him a roguish smile. The boy beside him gives a transparent laugh.

"Whoa! Twins!"

The clone leans over Jude's face. The Nigerian stands, runs to the sea and throws up. He washes his face. He throws up again, in violent convulsions, feeling like he might turn himself inside-out. "I've got my shoes wet," he thinks. "I'm going to ruin my shoes." He imagines himself turned inside-out. There's no way he can travel back to London inside-out, with his shoes ruined, his whole shirt stained with vomit. The police, at the border, will look at him, suspicious: "The thing is, senhor, you don't look remotely like the photo in the passport. And besides, those shoes . . ."

Somebody puts their arms around him from behind. Jude tries to breathe. He's scared to open his eyes. He hears the gentle voice of Luzia.

"Relax! I'll take you somewhere it's cooler."

Jude lets himself be led, eyes closed, feeling the weight of the sun on his face, the heat rising from the ground, pressing him and threatening to fling him through the air. And now, on top of the nausea, he also feels his stomach in knots, his guts dissolving, a pressing need to squat down in some corner and defecate.

6

Uli had been planning to attend Luzia and Ofélia's conversation at the art gallery of the Hotel Villa Sands, but when he walked past the library he decided to pop inside, feeling curious, and ended up missing the event. One of the employees, who was dozing, lying on a mat, recognised him. She got up, smiling, "Mr Writer, you're most welcome!" and made herself available to help in any way he needed. Uli thanked her. He only meant to have a quick peek inside. There was no-one else there. The faintest light came in through the only window, in the main hall, falling onto the old books on their tired shelves, barely illuminating their titles.

The writer sits on one of the chairs, his back to the window. He feels good there, amid the "great peace of books", as his father used to say. His father had been another poet, from whom he had learned to love libraries, the most destitute ones especially.

Uli gets up, walks over to the nearest bookcase and starts reading the titles. One of them catches his attention: *A Makua Drama – or a crime against nature*. He pulls out the slim volume with care. Its pages are still uncut. A virgin book, then, even in a small library with a very worn-out old collection. He thinks this extraordinary. He sits down at one of the tables, pulls a small penknife out of his rucksack and cuts the first few pages, feeling like an explorer opening up a path, with his katana, through a mysterious jungle. The penknife must be almost as old as the book. He's always carried it around with him, ever since he found it, by chance, left under a hotel bed. He uses it for peeling and cutting fruit. Less often, for, as in this instance, cutting the pages of old books that have never been read before. He's sorry they no longer sell books with their pages uncut. Libraries have been transformed into ready-to-read stores. The books are fast food. The ceremonial side of reading, in the old days, included the slow ritual of cutting the pages. There was no house with a library, small or large, that didn't have a paper knife. Shortly before his death, his father had given him one, a family heirloom, with a silver blade and ivory handle. To buy a paper knife like that nowadays, you'd have to search in a good antique store. Uli stretches out his legs and starts to read. First surprise: the action of the novel takes place on Ilha de Moçambique, in 1943. Second surprise: the main character is called Baltazar, like that tramp who dresses as a woman. Uli has a poor memory, but he had fixed the name in his mind because it was unusual and he thought it might be interesting for a character.

He reads without stopping, barely breathing, from the first page to the last. He gets up, uncertain. He shows the book to the librarian:

"May I take this to my hotel? I promise to bring it back tomorrow."

The woman agrees with a broad smile. The writer just needs to sign a bit of paper with his name and the number of an ID document.

Uli calculates that at that time Daniel will be in the Jardim dos Aloés, where they had agreed to go for an ice cream. He walks hurriedly. It is then that he sees Baltazar rushing across the street towards him.

7

Luzia has brought Jude to her room. The Nigerian writer is lying on the bed, still dressed but without shoes. The girl, standing, wipes his forehead with a damp towel.

"I've asked them to bring some coconut water. It'll do you good."

Jude wants to say something that might mend the discomfort of finding himself so wretched, so exposed, so helpless, on a woman's bed. However, the only words that occur to him are weak moans and clumsy apologies.

"Don't talk," says Luzia, "don't say anything."

She smiles inwardly – because she is privately pleased to have him there disarmed, dirty and human – without realising that her eyes betray her. Jude sees the brief flash and understands. He takes her right hand, pulls her towards him and kisses her. It is a crooked, bitter kiss, but Luzia responds with passion, climbing onto the bed, holding the back of Jude's neck, opening her lips to seek out Jude's tongue with hers.

They don't make it past that kiss because Jude suddenly leaps off the bed, runs out and locks himself in the bathroom. Luzia opens the big window onto the patio, shaking the infested air with a towel. She sees a guy on the beach, smiling at her. She runs to the bathroom door, and shouts.

"He's on the beach, he's looking this way."

"Who?" Jude tries to make his voice come out sounding firm, while he is suffering. "Wait. I'll be right there."

He cleans himself up, puts on his shorts and washes his hands. When he opens the door he doesn't see Luzia. He finds her on the terrace, her eyes turned towards the empty beach.

"He was right there. He was there a moment ago."

Jude hugs her.

"I believe you. I saw him earlier, too, next to the boat, when I started feeling ill."

"You think it was him?"

"No! Of course not. I ate something that was off."

"We've got to be more careful with the food. Lie down. I'll run you a hot bath."

Jude lies back down. Luzia sets the water running in the tub. She adds a few drops of eucalyptus oil. She smiles, while stirring the water. The temperature's good. She smells her hands. They smell good. Last night she'd dreamed about this, or rather, she'd dreamed they were having a bath together, her and Jude. In her dream, the tub was enormous. A pirogue drifted across the waters while the man caressed her.

"Come, the bath's ready!"

The Nigerian watches her, leaning against the door. Nobody would have guessed he was over forty. Even sick and haggard, with deep bags under his eyes, he looks like a boy. Some people's eyes never get old, Luzia thinks.

"What do you think is happening?" she asks him.

"On this island?"

"Yes, on this island . . ."

"We're cut off, with no means of communication and no power, because of a violent storm . . ."

"Violent and endless . . ."

"Violent and unending, like a punishment. Or like a blessing, depending on your perspective. I'm happy being here."

"With me?"

"Yes, with you. But a lot of people are nervous. Most of the hotels and restaurants don't have generators. That explains why some of the guest writers have fallen sick. Even I . . ."

"You're right. Ofélia woke up unwell, too . . ."

"That's what's happening. We're nervous and intoxicated. We're inclined to invent fantasies, to imagine situations that don't exist . . ."

"You seriously believe that?"

"I only believe what I can see. I believe in you."

"What are we going to do?"

"I'm going to take a bath. I really need one."

"Can I take a bath with you?"

Jude laughs.

"Save that for tomorrow?"

Luzia kisses his cheek.

"Of course. If you need anything, call me. They must be bringing the coconut water. Have a good bath, drink the coconut water and you'll feel better soon enough."

8

A huge Indian almond rises from the patio in the Jardim dos Aloés, casting an even, cool shade all around it. Uli Lima shuts his eyes. He is savouring a chocolate ice cream. The coolness of the almond tree calms him. The shade seems to mark out a border within which reality remains whole and reliable. Beyond it the city fades away, with its characters who've escaped from fiction, its collection of absurdities and impossibilities, bewildered people turning delirious in the sun.

"Well?!" asks Daniel, who saw him arriving minutes earlier, sweating and confused, waving a small red-covered book. "Are you going to tell me what happened? What book is that? Why didn't you show up at the gallery?"

Uli leans back in the chair. He inhales the renewed air, and thinks how different the city would be if every road had big trees like this one flourishing on them. He loves the world of plants. He can talk for hours about the particular history of each species – how the *Ficus religiosa* owes its name to Buddha, who found enlightenment in its miraculous shade; or about the *Vachellia xanthophloea*, better known as the fever tree, because it was believed for many years to cause malaria.

"Maybe it's the sun," he says at last. "The light can blind you more than darkness."

"What do you mean?"

Uli shakes his head. He holds the book as if it were a butterfly.

"Baltazar."

"The lunatic?"

"This book is the story of his life."

"Seriously?"

"Yes. The amazing thing is, it was published in 1949."

"So it's not our Baltazar."

"Unless our Baltazar is extremely well preserved . . ."

141

"So that's what you think, you think it's . . ."

Uli finishes his ice cream.

"The book's interesting. While it's typical colonial literature, with a view of the continent that's full of prejudices, the truth is that the author does make an effort to give the Africans a voice. This Baltazar was a washer-boy. He worked for a rich Portuguese trader, Adebaldo da Costa Cascudo, who set up here at the end of the nineteenth century and got rich exporting sisal, copra and sugar."

"Wait, is this a true story or fiction?"

"The book presents itself as a novel. Maybe it's based on real events that the author later fictionalised, I don't know."

"What's the writer's name?"

"Máximo Fortes. I'd never heard of him. He was a captain in the merchant navy. He quit his post after a serious accident, in which he lost an arm, and settled in Mozambique, producing tea. That's all I know about him. The book opens with a brief biographical note about the author."

"Right. So tell me the story about Baltazar."

"Baltazar was a washer-boy. He worked in the house of a rich Portuguese trader, sweeping, dusting, doing laundry, taking care of the vegetable garden and the grounds, helping to prepare meals. The trader had a fifteen-year-old son, Ricardo, a lad in delicate health, who was spoiled by his grandmother, protected by his mother and hated by his father. Ricardo admired Baltazar, because unlike him, the washer-boy was always cheerful, he responded to Adebaldo's insults with laughter and never allowed himself to be bowed. The friendship between the two irritated Adebaldo, who preferred to see his son playing football or exchanging blows with the other lads, instead of finding him smoking at the exit of the Imperial Cinema in the company of Baltazar, after they'd watched some Indian comedy or other. One night, when he found Ricardo teaching Baltazar to read, he became enraged, thrashed them both with a broad leather belt and finally threw the washer-boy out of the house. The boy didn't mind. The following day, the owner of the Imperial Cinema, a fat and pleasant old Goan man, offered him a job, his new duty being ensuring the cleanness of the cinema, as well as showing people to their seats and kicking out any free-loaders. Baltazar was delighted, as he could watch all the movies and he earned more than he had at Adebaldo's. Ricardo, meanwhile, became a huge movie buff. This lasted until the tragic night when Adebaldo came into his son's room, intending to have a serious conversation about the family business, and found him in bed, naked, with his arms around Baltazar, both of them so enraptured with each other that they only registered the man's presence when he, with a violent cry, tumbled senseless onto the floor. Baltazar fled to the mainland. He spent months in the bush, hopping from village to village, until one Sunday morning, when he had ventured into Lumbo, he met, coming out of the church, the owner of the Imperial Cinema. The man wanted to know what had happened to him, because he'd disappeared so suddenly, coinciding with the departure of the Costa Cascudo family to the mother country. Adebaldo, he told him, had suffered a coronary. He had lost the power of speech. He had boarded the steamship *Angola* in a wheelchair, pushed by Ricardo, who was looking very thin, very pale, with his mother and grandmother beside him. They never returned to Mozambique. Baltazar came back to the island, but since then he'd acquired the habit of dressing as a woman, always wearing the brightest and most beautiful kapulanas, and painting his face with mussiro."

"That's all in the book?" asked Daniel. "The thing about the mussiro, too?"

Yes, Uli nodded.

"Maybe this Baltazar is the son of the other one," the Angolan suggested. "You might find it became a family tradition for the eldest sons to inherit their father's name, to wear kapulanas, and paint their faces with mussiro."

"He came to me."

"Baltazar? When?"

"Just now, he saw me coming out of the library."

"And?"

"And he pointed at the book, and said: 'I was born from that book.'"

THE FIFTH DAY

Words hold up the sky.
Oh sky: give us beings who are kind.

JOB SIPITALI, *Roots Sing*

I

Daniel wakes up within the night, as if in a river, feeling the darkness dragging him far away – and he doesn't find Moira. He gets up, still drowsy. Lightning-flashes explode in the distance, on the mainland, cutting out the silhouettes of huge baobab trees. Perhaps his wife decided to go downstairs in search of a biscuit, a bread roll or a piece of fruit. Since becoming pregnant, she has formed the habit of waking up suddenly in the small hours of the morning, with a pressing hunger, and running to the kitchen to find whatever there was to eat.

Daniel makes his way down the wooden ladder. His wife isn't in the kitchen, nor in the living room, nor in the bedroom, nor in the study. He calls out to her, concerned. Nobody answers. He puts on a T-shirt, some shorts and a pair of sandals and goes out onto the street, picturing worst-case scenarios. He always does this whenever he fears something bad might happen. The future, he believes, is devised in such a way as to contradict any predictions. If we imagine some occurrence, in as much detail as possible, it almost never happens, or at least it never happens the way we imagined it.

And so, as he anxiously walks the streets of the sleeping

town, Daniel sees Moira leaping into the sea, being kidnapped by drug traffickers, getting run over by a drunk driver, pursued by packs of dogs.

The jetty is vanishing into the night. The writer turns on his phone torch and walks all the way to the end. He finds the cockroach-woman sitting on the cement steps that go down into the sea. She is naked. She gestures, as if beckoning him, but Daniel flees. When he finally realises where he is, he's standing in front of Lucília's house. He knocks on the door, calls her name. After a few minutes, the window opens and the writer recognises the sleepy face of the midwife's husband.

"Lucília took Moira to the hospital. They didn't tell you?"

The hospital?! The Ilha de Moçambique Hospital had once been among the biggest in Southern Africa, and the most beautiful. Abandoned in the years that followed independence, it sheltered refugees coming from the mainland, and was gradually eaten away, vandalised, devastated by storms, until little was left of it but the tall wounded façade, with its six elegant columns that make it look like a Greek temple (a ruined one). Moira wanted to have the baby at home. Daniel agreed. If there was any problem, they could go to the Nacala Hospital, just over an hour away. It never occurred to them to have the birth at the island hospital.

The writer runs off. In front of the doors to the houses, there are people sleeping, stretched out on mats. Occasionally, one of them raises their head when they see him pass. One boy shouts:

"Hey, tio Daniel!"

Daniel doesn't stop. He keeps running, leaping over sleepers, holes and loose stones, until finally, breathless now, he sees the venerable building's worn-out walls. He stops next to an old man, who looks like he's awaiting the end of days, sitting on a chair, under the big hospital gateway.

"Maternity ward?"

The old man gestures distractedly, waving towards a path round the back of the main building. The writer plunges through the darkness, making an effort not to trip in the holes. About fifty metres on, he spots a faint light. Guided by this, he climbs a few quick steps, up into a broad room occupied by a couple of dozen iron beds, very rusty now, most of them without mattresses. Two of the beds have mosquito nets. On one of them, covered by a grimy kapulana, lies a woman with a small, grim face, her dull little eyes fixed on the dirty ceiling. In the other, he can make out Moira, who looks like she's asleep, with her back to him. He walks towards her, trembling, and only then does he see the defenceless little head of the baby. He kneels down at the foot of the bed. Moira opens her eyes and smiles:

"So beautiful, isn't she?"

"What happened? Why didn't you tell me?"

"You were sleeping so well, my love. We didn't want to wake you."

The voices wake the girl, who turns towards her father with a crooked smile. Daniel pushes aside the mosquito net and holds her tiny little hand.

"So is she Tetembua?" he asks.

"Yes, you won. I want to get out of here. Take us home."

Lucília interrupts them.

"I can see Daddy's already met his daughter. Congratulations!"

Moira asks Lucília if she can leave the hospital. Lucília agrees and offers to take them in her car. She wraps the girl in a kapulana and hands her to Daniel. She helps Moira to get up and get dressed. Twenty minutes later, the couple is back home. Seeing as the bed is still set up on the terrace, they decide to spend the rest of the night on a wide charpai, which Moira had bought, badly damaged, for half a dozen meticals, and restored, adding a foam cushion with a kapulana cover. Little Tetembua, lying between the two of them, seeks out one of her mother's breasts, latches on to it and sucks.

2

The house fills with people, including many Daniel has never seen before. Moira is still locked in the bedroom, with the baby. She gave her husband stern instructions not to let anybody in. She repeated the same instructions to Momade de Jesus, whom she trusts much more than she does Daniel. The servant put a chair outside the bedroom door and sat down, rigid, silent, frowning, keeping watch over the party.

"Can't we see the girl?" asks Dona Francisca de Bragança, annoyed.

Moira refuses to see anybody at all, fearful that little Tetembua, who is now utterly exposed to the countless evils of the world, might contract some virus, bacteria, fungus, or be scared at the commotion of life. The future will quickly demonstrate the absurdity of this terror, since not only was Tetembua born with her body armoured against the worst illnesses, but she also showed herself the most curious and social of beings, loving noise, parties and crowds.

The writer sits down for a moment in the yard, in the shade of the lemon tree, and shuts his eyes, struggling to recover his breath. Laughter circles all around him. All the voices muddle into one euphoric racket. Daniel doesn't notice Uli arriving. His friend pulls over a chair and sits down next to him.

"Tired?"

Daniel opens his eyes.

"I've hardly slept."

"Just think, that was one of the more peaceful nights. The next ones will be much worse."

"Shit, give me a break!"

They are interrupted by a man with a dishevelled white beard, thick eyebrows on the rampage and a shy smile, who, after congratulating Daniel, greets Uli.

"You don't recognise me anymore?"

Uli jumps to his feet and hugs him.

"Ramiro, it's so good to see you!"

Ramiro Rendeiro has lived on the island for many long years, directing excavations, teaching at the university, writing and shepherding an old blind goose along the beaches, roads and squares of the town. A good, generous man, like a Christ who had opted to abdicate from Christianity, he dispersed his vast family fortune quietly and without fanfare, investing in scientific projects and helping those most in need. Uli likes him very much. He turns to Daniel.

"Remember that story I told you, about the bloodsuckers?"

"Yes, of course."

"Ramiro was in that group."

Ramiro remembers it well. Unlike the other scientists, who fled to Nampula, the archaeologist insisted on remaining on the island. He thought the rumours would disperse within a few days and that they would leave him in peace. That's not how it went. He began to get hassled. Children threw stones at him. One morning, he was awoken by a commotion. He looked out the window and saw a small crowd posted at his door. He phoned a friend of his, a retired surgeon, who ran over to help him. The doctor spent half an hour talking with the demonstrators, in Makua. Ramiro followed the discussion through a window, not understanding what they were saying. Finally his friend returned, looking very serious, to report on what was happening.

"Don't worry. The guys are pretty well resigned. They know you're a bloodsucker just like the others who ran away, and that you're going to attack them sooner or later. 'May Allah's will be done,' they say, 'may Allah's will be done.' They just demand that before you do any sucking, you make arrangements for at least some soup and a bit of buttered bread, as they're starving."

Ofélia bursts into the yard.

"There are clashes broken out between police and civilians, by the fish market," she says.

She herself has seen a police officer, with a head wound, going into the hospital. Júlio Zivane confirms this. One of the staff at the Terraço das Quitandas told him some fishermen disembarked on the island with a shipwrecked man they'd rescued from the middle of the sea. When the police arrived, intending to take the man away, the fishermen rose up. They wanted to hear him, to learn if he had any news of the mainland. One of the officers fired three shots in the air, which served only to inflame tempers all the more.

3

On the day he was named to head up the station on the Ilha de Moçambique, Juvêncio Baptista Nguane went back to the house where he was born, which had been sitting empty for five months, ever since the death of his mother, he locked himself in the kitchen and wept. He hadn't cried since he was fifteen, when a girl he was in love with departed for Johannesburg, leaving him with the absolute certainty that he would grow old alone, without a wife and with no children to take care of him. Locked in the kitchen, Juvêncio wept with anger and disgust, ranting against his arsehole of a boss, a corrupt, fat man, who had decided to punish him with a kind of exile, disguised as a promotion, to prevent him from investigating a famous drug dealer. His wife, however, received the news joyfully: "You're going to earn more, and spend more time with your family," she told him. "Our children are going to grow up with a father. I'll have my husband back."

Juvêncio imagined that, banished to the island, he would die of boredom long before retirement. He was wrong. He's been awake three days now, trying to put the world in order. At least, the narrow world that it falls to him to govern. In front of him, wrapped in a kapulana with the image of President Samora Machel, stands a haggard, astonished young man, who claims his name is Calamity. The commander writes this name down in a large notebook.

"You were born in 2000, am I right?"

"2000, yes, boss."

"During the great floods . . ."

"My mother says I was born in the water, with the fishes."

"And now you almost die in the water."

"Yes, boss, with the fishes."

The commander shakes his head, impressed with God's propensity, or fate's, for tragic irony. He gets up from his desk, resisting the temptation to give the young man a hug. If it were up to him, he would solve all humanity's problems with hugs, kisses and pats on backs. He walks over to the window. He sees the populace gathering at the station doors. He sits back down.

"So what happened, Senhor Calamity?"

"The world ended."

"The world has not ended, Calamity. Here we are, the two of us, talking, on Ilha de Moçambique, so the world has not ended."

"It's all water, boss. Out there, on the other side, the houses have turned into water, the trees into water, the people into water. Even the light and the air are made of the same endless water of the end of the world."

Juvêncio takes a deep breath. If he frees Calamity and the young man leaves the station, the people will quickly surround him asking for information. The man will repeat what he's just said to him, that the world's ended and there's nothing but water and dead earth mixed with sea, beyond the horizon. Calamity's testimony will increase the population's nervousness even further. He explains to the young man that he's going to have to keep him in one of the cells, until the storm is calmed and everything goes back to normal. Calamity receives the verdict with a broad smile. He just doesn't want to be sent back to the water.

4

Daniel has asked the writers, journalists and other guests to gather at the Terraço das Quitandas, at 3 p.m., to discuss the latest events. About thirty people are waiting for him on the veranda, settled into the armchairs, in hammocks or on cushions, many of them fanning themselves. It was Moira's idea to order the fans from a local craftsman, giving them to the participants along with a full programme of events. As soon as Daniel comes in, followed by Uli, Cornelia gets up and confronts him.

"My flight's today! I want to leave!"

Daniel steps in to kiss her, but she pulls her face away.

"Where's my car?"

The Angolan steps back, takes a deep breath and, turning to the other guests, apologises on behalf of the organisation for all the setbacks. The island is still cut off. There is no news from the mainland. It's impossible to say when communication will resume. Meanwhile, they should remain in their respective hotels.

"Is it dangerous to go out?" asks Jussara Rabelo.

Several people put up their hands. Some of them want to report violent or strange events they have witnessed in the last few days. Others have complaints. Some hotels have run out of fuel for their generators and without air conditioning it's almost impossible to breathe in the bedrooms, there's no beer on sale anywhere, etc.

Uli calls for silence. He speaks to everyone, as if addressing each individually, with the same voice he uses, as legend would have it, for hypnotising elephants, explaining that this is an extraordinary situation and that it will soon be resolved. Let's just imagine we're on holiday, he says, and make the most of the sun and the sea. For those who don't like sun or sea, and much less holidays, make the most of the time to read and write, or just to chat with one another, as I've been doing, surrounded by writers I've admired for so many years and by friends I see less often than I'd like. Chained to our everyday responsibilities, we're always complaining we don't have time for the simple things in life. Well, then – now we have time.

"Being married to Uli has got to be a feminist's worst nightmare," Ofélia murmurs to Luzia. "The guy opens his mouth and I forget all my principles. I'd live on my knees, at his feet, serving him like a slave."

Luzia laughs.

"I think he's like one of those circus magicians who distracts the respectable audience with one hand while tricking them with the other."

Jude gets up.

"Uli's right. We need to help one another. Live in the moment. Let's pretend we're shipwrecks."

"We're shipwrecks!" shouts Júlio Zivane.

"Fine," says Pedro Caminha. "We're shipwrecks. We'll live like shipwrecks. But on what? I've spent the morning talking to fishermen. They say there are fewer and fewer fish in the sea. They can't explain it. Already there's hardly anything fresh to be had in the market. It's all stuff in tins."

Daniel's talked to the fishermen, too. He's talked to the owners of the hotels and the main restaurants. Everyone's complaining about the lack of produce: potatoes increasingly hard to come by, vegetables getting smaller and smaller, the last of the chickens costing a fortune. At low tide, the expanse of sand is filled with women and children, with a knife in one hand and a basin in the other, hunting for sea urchins and bivalves.

Once again, Uli comes out in Daniel's defence.

"We're not going to starve to death. It's true that the fishermen are complaining about the lack of fish, but they haven't stopped fishing. The restaurants are still open. They're serving lunch and dinner. Yes, it's hard to find vegetables at the market, but there's no shortage of chocolate."

"Or coffee!" shouts Jude. "And as long as there's coffee, I'm not giving up."

Some laughter. Then Júlio Zivane stands up.

"Shall we talk about the characters?"

"What characters?" asks Daniel, tense.

"You know very well!" shouts Zivane. "Our characters. You can't open a book on this fucking island without some character escaping and running off to live on the street. And no, I'm not drunk. I haven't touched a drop in two days . . ."

A brief confusion breaks out. The Togolese writer Sami Tchak says he had coffee that morning with Jude's literary double, at Pontão, watching the storm swallow up the final memories of the mainland. Jude replies that he ought to have chucked him into the sea, that other Jude, who might have brought him fame and profit to begin with, but now brings him shame. Ofélia swears that she met Dona Epifânia, at the market, seducing the kapulana-sellers. Jussara wants to know if there's a candomblé house anywhere on the island. Pedro Caminha asks if anyone else has seen the cockroach-woman. Cornelia gets up and quits the veranda, yelling, complaining about the heat and about her colleagues' insanity and promising never to come back to Mozambique again.

At this moment, Moira comes in, crossing paths with Cornelia. The Nigerian woman brushes her brusquely aside, before disappearing into the hallway. Daniel runs over to hug his wife.

"What are you doing here?"

Moira releases him from the hug. The writers get up to meet her. They applaud, kiss her, congratulate her. Some ask how the birth went. Others want to know what the girl is called. She ignores them. She takes a small copper bell out from her handbag and shakes it energetically, fierce and shrill, until everyone has stopped talking.

"Calm down, people! It's not the end of the world."

Or maybe it is, she adds. The world is wiped out every moment. And every moment it re-begins. For example, just a few hours ago, a beginning of the world happened right there, on the island, in her life, in the lives of so many around her. On the other hand, she remembers having looked at the sky, on her way to the hospital, and being surprised at how empty the night was. The stars are disappearing, just like the fish in the sea, the insects and the birds in the sky, or that narrow thread of land, the horizon, with the silhouette of the great baobabs, which we all believe eternal. She doesn't know what's happening. A magnificent dream. A nightmare. A marvellous illusion. All these at once, or maybe just the universe exercising its mysteries. And then there are the characters, Moira continues, there are the characters coming out of books and occupying the streets. She herself saw Cornelia Oluokun's cockroach-woman, and she has talked to, or tried to talk to, Jude D'Souza's arrogant alter-ego.

She pauses, briefly, to take a breath. Instantly a new turmoil rises up, everybody talking at once, until Moira rings the bell again.

"For fuck's sake, shut up!"

The writers fall silent.

"We're the ones who construct the worlds," Moira continues. "It's us! The worlds germinate in our heads, and grow till they don't fit anymore, and then they burst loose, drop into the world and put down new roots. That's reality, it's what happens to fiction when we believe in it!"

5

Lying on the bed, her face buried in the mattress and a pillow over her head, Cornelia doesn't hear Moira's speech. Her body is liquefying from the heat. She's heard something about a shipwreck, a poor upholsterer rescued from the sea by fishermen, who claims to have witnessed the end of the world. The upholsterer saw his whole family transformed into water. He tried to save his little girl, grabbed hold of her, clutched her to his chest, and she drained unstoppably through his trembling fingers.

Cornelia is also about to change state. When they come into her room the following morning, they'll find her bedsheets soaked. Someone will say: "Hey look, that Nigerian cow's gone – she's turned into water." They'll hang the sheets out to dry on one of the terraces until she has completely evaporated. She thinks about Pierre. She can see him running around the island, looking for her, breathing her, stopping when he recognises her bitter scent.

A series of small clicks awakes her from her daydreaming. She turns over in bed and opens her eyes. Lucy, the cockroach-woman, is sitting in front of her. She's cracking her wrists and knuckles, with her eyes fixed on the floor. The writer jumps out of bed and presses herself against the opposite wall, gauging the distance between herself and the door.

"How did you get in here?" she murmurs in Yoruba.

Lucy lets her head fall back, like a disarticulated doll. She rolls her eyes.

"I flew in, through the window." She gives a little laugh, which wounds the writer like an insult.

"What do you want from me?"

The cockroach-woman inhales the dense air of the bedroom. She needs to understand who she is, where she came from. Where she'll go after the end. Cornelia looks at her in a troubled silence, moves closer.

"I don't know," she admits. "I never know where any of you come from. There are so many nights inside me! There's so much darkness!"

She says this and then she cries, trying to hide her tears

with her hands, but Lucy gets up and takes her fingers and kisses them.

"I'm scared, mother, I'm scared. What's to become of me?"

Cornelia is scared, too. She, too, needs to understand who she is, and where she has come from, and where she will go when everything has ended.

"I gave you a companion, someone who was like you," she says. "To protect you. For you to protect. For you to love each other."

"Max," murmurs the cockroach-woman. "His name is Max."

Lucy gets up, opens the bedroom door and goes out into the hallway. She closes the door. Cornelia stays for some time, sitting on the bed. Then, finally, she gets up, sits at the desk, opens her laptop and begins to write:

It rained so much that the water covered the world. Only one island was saved, built entirely on a solid block of pumice stone that insisted on floating upon the waters, with its solid Portuguese fortress, the big colonial houses, the dazzling Arab terraces, the churches and chapels and mosques, and fifteen thousand souls suffering under an air so heavy and humid that early some mornings even the frogs drown in it. A long rope bridge, with a wooden handrail, connected the island to the mainland. Before the storm, the bridge served to connect one land to the other but also to prevent the island from breaking loose and drifting off to sea and disappearing, never to be seen again. After the rains, anybody intending to cross the bridge would no longer find terra firma, but a very vast, lost territory, which the islanders call, simply, out of laziness, the end of the world.

One afternoon, a boy crossed the bridge, carrying a bucket in his right hand and a shovel in his left. When he reached the far side he went on, though it was very hard going, buried up to his knees in that material neither liquid nor solid, which seemed to be composed as much of the sea as of the lukewarm wreckage of the sky. He climbed a small hill and set about digging up the dead clouds, the decaying stars, the shrivelled remains of rainbows that had once adorned the dazzling sky. Noori, that was the boy's name, worked all afternoon. When the sun began its descent, he saw there was a large leaf in the shovel, lacy brown, with no life left in it at all – and yet, still a leaf. He knelt down and cried.

Noori took the leaf back to the island. He showed it to his best friend, The Bean, who had mocked him when he'd told him he would cross the bridge to dig up traces of life at the end of the world. The Bean held the leaf, studied it, sniffed it, and finally he gave in.

"Tomorrow I'll go with you."

The following morning, they both went.

They dug together, in a stubborn silence, until at around three in the afternoon the shovel hit something solid – and it was earth. The boys rejoiced. They returned to the island carrying their buckets filled with that dark matter, saved from the waters, and showed it to their parents. The parents, too, were moved and amazed. They called the neighbours, somebody brought drums and rattles, and soon the whole island was dancing and singing, in a party the like of which had not been seen in so long.

In the months that followed, the whole population mobilised to dig up the mainland, which they did metre by metre, in a heroic effort, first opening up a broad stretch of beach, on which they planted coconut palms and casuarinas. Then they advanced *inland, planting baobabs, banyan figs, cashew trees, mango trees, avocado trees, cocoa trees, banana trees, pitanga trees, tamarind and papaya trees; sowing beans, corn and millet. When they had become covered in leaves, the cashew trees, the fig trees, the mango trees and the avocado trees began to produce fruit, and soon after that, birds, hundreds of birds of every species, bee-eaters, partridges, larks, swallows, thrushes, starlings, waxbills, long-tailed tyrants, canaries and then eagles, falcons, crows, marabous, herons and storks, which took charge of propagating the seeds of these trees, spreading the green and conquering more and more land at the end of the world.*

Five years after Noori first crossed the bridge alone, carrying a bucket in one hand and a shovel in the other, there was only a little bit of the end of the world left, on the furthest corner of the continent, which the people decided to leave intact, in all its desolate impossibility, so that those to come would never doubt that, once, the sky had fallen onto the earth.

They say that when Noori died, all the birds came to the funeral, to say goodbye to him, and there were so many wings in the sky that the ground of the cemetery was covered in feathers, so people felt as though they were walking on shredded clouds.

Cornelia stops writing and only then does she notice that night has fallen. She shuts down her laptop and goes out onto the terrace. She does not see one single star.

6

Luzia and Jude are lying on their backs on the deck, beside the swimming pool, the woman resting her head on the man's chest.

"Look," says Jude, pointing at the sky. "A star has lit up now, there, right above us."

Luzia points at another, to the side.

"There are already two! No, three!"

The Nigerian strokes her face.

"The clouds are opening up," he murmurs.

"Either that, or someone's creating new stars by the dozen!" laughs Luzia.

"Some writer, going by Moira's theory. One of us, sitting in front of a notebook, or at a computer, rewriting the world."

"I like your hand." Luzia takes his hand and kisses it. "I like this hand that creates worlds."

"I need to tell you something. I should have told you before."

"What is it?"

"There's somebody waiting for me in London. A boyfriend."

Luzia sits up. She looks at him, embarrassed.

"I'm sorry, I hadn't realised."

Jude kneels next to her. He tries, unsuccessfully, to take her hands.

"It's not what you think. I mean, yes, I have a boyfriend. I live with an English actor. But I have had girlfriends, too. But in any case . . ."

Luzia gets up. She moves away.

"I don't know what to say."

"I'm sorry I hurt you so badly."

"No, you haven't done anything."

Jude gets up, seeing himself from somewhere on a slightly higher plane, and it's as if the person getting up is not him but a stranger, and with this he becomes aware of the ridiculousness of the situation. Still, he goes after Luzia, trips, almost falls.

"Listen, Luz, listen," he says, not knowing what to say, as he grabs her arm. And the moment she turns around, he kisses her on the lips. "I don't want to lose you."

Luzia takes three steps towards the sea. She notices that a good part of the sky, above them, is now covered in stars. The universe celebrating, she thinks, and here she is, suffering because of a man. She turns around.

"I'm going to sleep. We'll talk tomorrow."

Jude allows himself to collapse onto the deck, his face downturned towards the sea, which is right there, practically licking his hands, and which suddenly seems to him to be a very fat, smooth animal watching him, studying him, the way an entomologist would analyse a rare beetle. He gets up and leaves the hotel, walking fast, almost running, towards the Terraço das Quitandas.

7

The night is getting lighter as Jude walks. When he reaches the Largo da Alfândega he hears footsteps behind him. He turns and sees the other Jude, standing there, staring at him with eyes that are his and that are not, since he has never seen them like this before, these other eyes of his, laughing like mocking children.

"Seems she likes me more than you," says the copy.

The writer clenches his fists. He feels a sudden loathing towards himself, for not having talked to Luzia earlier, for not having told her that those few days on the island had transformed him and he no longer wants his former life, including England, with its dark days and its umbrellas dripping on the stairs, and Jon, always so polite, always so fierce in his defence of the needy and of good causes, always so blond and so tediously predictable, and even that damn novel in which he no longer recognises himself and which, nevertheless, has been transformed into his public face. Jude wants a fight, he wants to feel that kind of furious euphoria that happens when a heavy fist hits you hard, and nothing matters any longer but bringing your opponent down before he brings you down. Jude, the character, certainly read his thoughts, since while the writer's fist draws a beautiful half-ellipse in the motionless air, the former has already turned his face away with the delicate elegance of a dancer, and is now two steps back, laughing loud and resonant.

"Sit down," the creature tells his creator. "We're going to talk."

He sets an example, sitting on a small wooden bench. Jude, the real one, takes his place on the bench opposite. They face one another, the man and his character. The former tense, scowling. The latter, smiling with the grandeur of a prince visiting the savage provinces.

"Relax," says Jude, the character. "I am here to free you."

The writer regrets having quit tobacco three years earlier. This would be a good moment to pull out a cigarette, put it between his lips, and light it to inhale the smoke, giving him the time to recover his calm and clarify his reason. But instead he opens his arms, in a sign of surrender, sighs and just says:

"Talk!"

The other leans over him.

"If God was a fish, crocodiles wouldn't have teeth."

Jude remembers that the character in his novel *Such a Dark Light* is keen on proverbs. He irritates his interlocutors with his insistence on summarising every situation with a Yoruba saying. He, Jude, had had great fun while writing the book, inventing proverbs with an apparent African resonance. One French critic had drawn attention to the influence of all that incredibly rich African oral literature on the author's novel, basing his observation on this use of adages. Jude and his friends had laughed a great deal at the man's naïveté.

"I don't know what you mean by that."

"Oh, yes, you do . . ."

A huge goose emerges from the shadows and places itself between the two of them. Behind it comes Ramiro Rendeiro. He flops heavily down onto the bench, next to Jude, dishevelling the night with his dazzlingly white beard.

"OK?"

Jude remembers having been introduced to Ramiro that morning, at Moira's house. He holds out his hand.

"Is the goose yours?"

"Destiny. His name's Destiny. He's blind . . ."

"I get it . . ."

"Oh no, it wasn't me who gave him that name. I would never have given him that name. I'm no poet, no philosopher. I'm an archaeologist. It was my wife Alice who started calling him that. And it stuck."

He gives no indication of having noticed Jude, the character. He offers an assurance that the storm, on the mainland, has been losing strength. In two or three days, he will start diving again. He can't wait. It could be that the swell, close to the coast, has exposed the wreckage of some other buried ship. Most discoveries are accidental. Years earlier, he says, travelling by boat along the coast, he and Alice found a small house built next to an isolated bay. The place had no other trace of any human presence. The nearest main road was more than thirty kilometres away. They were curious, and came onto land at the beach and knocked on the door. The man who opened it was a former air-force pilot. During the civil war he'd flown a MIG-21, which was brought down by the guerrilla forces and crashed into the sea. The pilot had parachuted to safety.

"My plane's somewhere out there," he said, pointing to the ocean.

As soon as the war ended, the pilot had built a house in the same place where he'd almost lost his life. In the evenings he sits in a chair on the veranda, keeping vigil over the ocean, watching over the sleep of his old winged companion. Ramiro agreed to go diving, to see whether he might find any trace of the craft. He didn't. He did, however, find a seventeenth-century galleon.

The goose listens to the story right through to the end, then it raises its head, gives a fierce honk and hurls itself at something, in the stuffy mystery of the night. Ramiro gets up.

"Off I go after Destiny," he says, and leaves.

"Interesting story, the one about the pilot," murmurs Jude, the character.

The writer agrees with a slight nod.

"I think God's a crocodile."

8

Back in his room, Jude discovers he's forgotten to leave his laptop plugged in. In the meantime, the generator's been switched off. The computer battery only has two per cent charge. He goes out and sits on the veranda with a notebook and a Montblanc pen, a gift from Jon. By the hesitant light of a candle, he begins to write:

When the builder of castles opened his eyes, he was still in the very same place. He couldn't have said how long he'd been there. Nor could he have said whether time existed in the place where he was. Days and nights did not follow one another. And nor did the animals and trees develop, or bodies grow old. The builder of castles had shut his eyes long enough for the grasses to grow and swallow everything up, and when he opened them again, he found the world just the same. The plentiful cool shade of the mulemba, a happy aroma, a river flowing in the background and its slow murmuring.

However long he walked, and he had already walked a long way, he couldn't leave the mulemba's shade. The river was still there, stuck to the horizon, sparkling, apart from everything, like a mirage. Only the visitors changed.

At that moment, on opening his eyes, he found a small boy standing before him.

"Who are you?" he asked.

"I'm the boy who sold peanuts," the boy replied. "And who are you?"

"I'm the builder of castles. I built castles."

"Amazing! And what did you build castles for?"

"To protect the princes."

"Protect them from who?"

"From other princes."

"And those other princes, did they have castles, too?"

"Yes, they had castles, too."

"And did you build castles for all the princes?"

"For those who could pay. Castles are expensive. I learned how to build castles from my father. In my family we've been building castles for several generations."

The boy sat down on the sand, beside the builder of castles. He looked at him, friendly.

"Where were you before you appeared here?"

"I was right here, in the shade of this same mulemba," the boy replied. "There's no way to leave the shade of the mulemba. There's not even any way to climb the mulemba. You climb and climb and you're always just in the same place. If we did manage to climb the mulemba, we'd be able to look out beyond the river. Here only the people change. We close our eyes and the people change. Isn't that what it's like for you?"

"Yes," agreed the builder of castles, "I think it's like that for everyone, but I do make a point of repeating the question because *it could be that someone else has a different story to tell. What do you think there is beyond the river?"*

"I don't think there's anything."

"I don't think even the river itself exists, it's just an image."

"Could be. Otherwise, what's the point of a river if we can't touch its water?"

They both looked out, contemplating the horizon for a long moment. Then the builder of castles said:

"And what about us? Do we really exist?"

"We do exist!" the boy assured him. "We do exist, though not really. If we really existed, we would feel pain."

"Pain? I feel pain!"

"Does your stomach hurt?"

"No, my stomach doesn't hurt."

"Does your head hurt?"

"No, my head doesn't either. What hurts is my past."

"Oh, the past! The past exists without existing, just like that river. You think it's there, you can see it, but you can't dive into it. Nobody can just dive straight into the past."

"I don't know. The river waters don't disappear. They just move place. Maybe something similar happens with the days we leave behind us: they aren't wiped out, they are concealed somewhere else."

The boy didn't answer. He was distracted watching the clouds. They spun slowly, high in the sky, now very white, now golden, now a soft pink colour. The boy yawned, and lay back. He turned to the builder of castles and smiled.

"Sorry, my friend, I'm going to shut my eyes now."

He shut his eyes and disappeared.

The strangest person the builder of castles met in the shade of the mulembas was not even a person – it was a cow. Out of politeness, and by force of habit, the builder of castles asked it, as he asked all visitors:

"Who are you?"

The cow didn't answer. It looked at him, bored. An ancient weariness, which the builder of castles felt as an insult. It shut its eyes and disappeared.

The builder of castles, alone again, started to build castles out of sand. It was something he did with admirable skill, even though, in the process, his memory would ache. He was doing this when he heard, behind him, a woman's voice, slow, slightly hoarse: they're lovely, your castles. Shame they're made of sand. They're not going to last long.

The builder of castles turned and saw a dark-skinned, slender young woman, with a dress that looked too opulent, or at least too red, to be wearing in the shade of a mulemba.

"Castles last as long as dreams," he replied, "the blink of an eye."

The woman laughed.

"Yes, I suppose so, senhor. Who are you?"

"I am the builder of castles."

"You think people are what they do?"

The builder of castles thought a moment.

"What we do makes us, yes. Nevertheless, we should be more than just a profession. Unfortunately, I believe I've only been a builder of castles my whole life. I've never been able to be any more than that."

The woman shook the elegant architecture of her shoulders with a very pure laugh.

"Would you like to know what I did?"

"What?"

"I was an actress. I pretended to be other people. That's while I was working. After a certain point, out of a professional bad habit, out of fear, I can't say for sure, I started pretending I was another person, or other people, even when I was far from the stage."

"Out of fear?"

'Fear that others wouldn't like who I really was. So I started performing other people. It's easier being many than just one. Being only one seemed such a responsibility! Since I've always had a talent for acting, I'm good at it, other people believed I was those people. From time to time, in private, I still happened to be myself. I happened to be myself out of pure absent-mindedness."

"And now?"

"Now, here?"

"Yes, here. In the shade of this mulemba."

"I talk to people to try to find out who I am. I think, if I discover who I am, this dream will end and I'll wake up somewhere I know."

"I'd never thought of that possibility," admitted the builder of castles, interested. "However, I don't think we're trapped inside a dream. Dreams are short and disorganised, sometimes we're a fly, other times the chameleon that swallows it. This place seems rather different to me. It's a coherent location, albeit an absurd one. I don't believe I'm going to wake up, sometime soon, in my own bed. I reckon we've died. We're all dead."

"We're dead?"

"We're dead. Maybe we have been for some time. For a little while or for ages, makes no difference."

The actress got scared. Or pretended to get scared. Her eyes slightly open, her breathing accelerated. There was no way of knowing whether she was pretending or she really had got scared, since she was, after all, a good actress.

"I can't imagine being dead. I've never played a dead woman."

"I think we are dead. I think we are dead, and that we've wound up here, in this madness, as a punishment. We're here to suffer."

"In hell? Do you think we are in hell?"

"Call it what you like."

The actress smiled. Her smile, thought the builder of castles, this alone denied the possibility of hell. Moreover, you didn't feel the weight of time here. Whereas in hell, the damned must feel the weight of time, the whole time. Hell is the weight of time.

"Maybe I am already dead," the woman said, "but I don't feel like I'm in hell. I just feel lost, like a child who's let go of her mother's hand in a crowd. I've let go of my own hand. Here I wander, rather distressed, waiting for this dream to end. In the meantime, I meet interesting people. I like talking to them. I'm not in hell, not even in a nightmare. When I meet somebody I don't like, I need only close my eyes."

"Please don't close them now," said the builder of castles. "Talk to me a little longer."

He wanted to see her smile again. His past ached less when she smiled. Unfortunately, he didn't know how to make her smile. In life, or in his other form of life, the builder of castles had been an austere man. The monks had taught him to distrust smiles. Laughter enraged him. Happiness seemed an unpleasant carelessness on the part of coarse brutes, or worse still, a sign of disrespect, almost an insult, towards the Lord Jesus, who died on a wooden cross to save mankind. Now, however, he was no longer sure that was the case. He had almost completely lost his faith in Jesus. He had lost his faith in whatever. He was thinking about this, about the dizziness of his past life, about the faith he had lost, when the woman, without his saying a thing, smiled again.

"I'm here," she murmured. "I've never met a builder of castles before. Did you like building castles?"

The builder of castles got excited. Oh yes, since he was a boy. He used to see his father designing castles. Then he would see them rising up from the mud with great effort, in an asthmatic struggle, in a straining of blind pachyderms, until they were transformed gradually into what his father had dreamed.

"Castles are always built against something, against others," remarked the woman. "That didn't bother you?"

"On the contrary. Castles are built to protect people."

"Very well, I understand. Nevertheless, they are built for war. Castles tend to attract wars, the same way the happiness of a bride and groom converges towards churches."

"That and the sadness of funerals."

"Yes, you're right." The young woman laughed.

The builder of castles sighed.

"I've lived through wars, through dark times. I was complicit in atrocities. But what could I do? I was only the builder of castles."

The actress took his hand. She held it between hers.

"At least you lived a life of your own. It was whole, getting things right sometimes and wrong others, being magnificent and contemptible. I, meanwhile, lived others' lives, dozens of them, more truthfully than my own. And anyway, what actually happened to mine?"

"Don't exaggerate. You surely were loved. You surely loved somebody."

"Yes, but I loved better when I was pretending to love, using words that someone wrote for me and believing in them more than in those that occurred to me when I was myself. When I was myself, every phrase sounded weak, ridiculous, totally artificial. Let's be honest, life is rarely elegant."

The builder of castles smiled. An awkward, slightly cock-eyed smile, the smile of somebody who hadn't smiled since childhood.

"Life is always elegant when you're nearby."

The actress looked at him, surprised, shut her eyes and disappeared. The builder of castles thrust out his right hand, as if wanting to clutch on to her, but it was too late. In the distance, the river slid by, indifferent. Birds he couldn't see sang amid the dense foliage. The man closed his eyes. When he reopened them, he found, standing before him, a lion-tamer. After the lion-tamer came a hairdresser, three primary-school teachers, a general, forty-four Indian merchants, a hundred and thirty Chinese merchants. The builder of castles asked them all whether, by any chance, they had met, there beneath the shade of the mulemba, an actress in a red dress. One of the Chinese merchants had met an actress. He remembered her well, a woman with fleshy lips and breasts that seemed to levitate. She'd been a big star in porn movies. The builder of castles wanted to know what porn movies were. The merchant's enthusiasm didn't make him feel the same way, on the contrary. He shut his eyes, appalled, and when he reopened them he found, before him, sitting on a stone, a fattish man, who stared at him with that mistaken, directionless look that blind men fix on things.

"Are you blind, senhor?" asked the builder of castles.

"I was blind, yes," said the man. "I was a blind writer. Writing helped me to see. Now that I see but do not write, I feel I see less well."

"What did you use to write about?"

'About what I didn't know about. It's only worth writing about what we don't know, about what terrifies us. I wrote about dreams, about death, about time."

"Well, senhor, you're in the right place, then."

The writer agreed. He closed his eyes and he was immediately replaced by a sailor with his legs crossed, his back very straight. He wore a little ring in his left ear. Before the builder of castles was able to ask him anything, the sailor held out his hand and pointed to the river.

"You know what's missing there?"

The builder of castles looked at him, surprised.

"Where? At the river?"

"Yes, at the river."

"What's missing?"

"A bridge!"

"A bridge?"

"Clearly, a bridge. How are we to get over to the other side?"

The builder of castles couldn't hide his annoyance. He raised his voice.

"We're never going to get over to the other side. There is no other side."

The sailor laughed. There was no malice in his laughter.

"Of course there is. The river exists, this side exists, the bank we're on, and so does the other. All rivers have two banks. That means we must cross it and reach the far side."

"We must?!"

"Yes! If the river's there, it's for us to cross it."

The builder of castles gestured wearily at the ample shade surrounding them.

"The shade of this mulemba is our prison. There's no way out of here."

The sailor jumped to his feet, startling the other man.

"The shade is only a prison when it prevents us from seeing. I've been in many prisons. None with such a fine view. A jail with a view like this can never be a place of penance, it's a delightful trick."

"And do you believe in hell, senhor?"

"Of course, but it's an internal place. One doesn't go to hell, one doesn't go to paradise. We go wherever we go, with them. We carry them inside us. There are people who grow the hell they carry within them. In others, a paradise grows in their heads. Many never develop either one. Those are the most unhappy, for they have never lived."

"And in God?"

"In God?"

"Do you believe in God?"

"What for?"

He leaned over and held out his hand, which the builder of castles shook gravely.

"It's been a pleasure talking to you, senhor. I wish you happy encounters and an excellent day. I hope we meet again on the other side of the river."

He shut his eyes and disappeared.

"Wow," murmured the builder of castles to himself, "what a curious character."

He could still feel his heart pounding. At the same time, he *regretted the sailor's sudden departure. He also regretted not having had more time to chat to the writer. The best conversations, he thought, are those that make us uneasy, that raise our heart-rate. He spent a long moment contemplating what the sailor had said about bridges, about hell and about God. He had spent his entire life building prisons, or fighting other men in the name of an absent God. He remembered the soldiers advancing against the ramparts. Those were the last images he remembered. The smell of boiling oil being poured. The screams of the wounded, the blaze of the flames, the furious din of metal against metal.*

"I should have built bridges!" he shouted.

"I built bridges."

The builder of castles turned around and found a pale, thin woman behind him, exceptionally blonde, her hair giving off sparks, her eyes filled with a springtime light.

"I built a lot of bridges," the woman said, walking nervously around the builder of castles. "I loved my work. From a certain point, however, I allowed myself to be overtaken by arrogance and I started building bridges out of vanity, like one of those writers who write not so as to see better but so as better to be seen. What happened to me was what always happens when we lose our passion: one of my bridges collapsed. A lot of people died. My career was over."

She sat down on the ground, beside the builder of castles. They sat there, the two of them, in silence, while out in the distance, in her past, the bridge was collapsing, dragging people down with it. Finally the builder of castles spoke up:

"Would you teach me to build bridges?"

The engineer of bridges smiled.

"Nothing would make me happier!"

She went to fetch a twig and began drawing in the sand. Years went by, or something resembling years, since, as I've already said, there was no time in that condition or state or circumstance of souls, and the two of them went on doing calculations and devising bridges. Finally, the engineer of bridges stretched out on her back, her blonde hair burning slowly, eyes lost amid the eternal foliage.

"There is nothing more I can teach you. You've shown yourself to be a good student. Now you know as much as me. Now you are, like me, an engineer of bridges."

She said this and shut her eyes. The builder of castles, or rather, the engineer of bridges, stood up happy. He stretched. It seemed to him that the river was singing. On that day – day being one way of putting it – he was visited by at least a dozen workmen and merchants, a surgeon, a lutenist, a worm-breeder and a mathematician. He asked all of them if they had encountered an actress in a red dress. While he'd been learning to build bridges, with the same youthful passion he'd learned to build castles, he had never stopped thinking about her. The image of the actress filtered like an inaugural light through the cracks of his inattention. He had only to become distracted for a moment for her liquid laughter to throw him into disarray. However, none of those people had met the woman. The engineer of bridges asked the mathematician if there was any possibility of seeing her again. The mathematician creased his ample brow in a frown.

"It would be a remarkable coincidence. Or rather – why not? Being alive means anything's possible."

Moments later, a woman as long and flexible as a snake, a yoga teacher, was even more optimistic:

"You just need to learn to open your eyes. Each time you

open them you find a new person before you, right? Then open them more times. Keep opening them, thinking about the person you'd like to meet."

A whole crowd paraded under the shade of the mulemba, and from each of these people the engineer of bridges learned something. He saw the cow again that he'd met a long time before. That cow or another, the engineer of bridges couldn't swear it was the same one. This time, the animal looked at him, not with displeasure, but with tenderness. Then it spoke, with a voice that wasn't a cow's voice, but an old turtle's:

"On the other side of the river, the grazing is better."

With these words it shut its eyes and disappeared. The engineer of bridges had never paid any attention to cows before. He was quite struck, though, by the authority with which it had spoken. The words would have seemed irrelevant to him, especially in the mouth of a cow, had it not been for the tone it had used. Tone is almost always more important than what's said. The engineer of bridges shut his eyes. When he reopened them, he found himself standing before the resplendent laugh of the actress in the red dress.

"You?"

The actress clapped her hands, happily.

"I've been looking for you."

The engineer of bridges had been preparing himself for this meeting for several eternities. On seeing her, however, he realised that he would never be prepared. His hands trembled. He struggled to breathe. He was frank:

"When you get near to me, I feel the air thinning. Taking a breath becomes difficult. And so, with my brain deprived of oxygen, I suffer attacks of stupidity, I lose my reason, I don't know, I say things that just aren't quite right."

181

The actress silenced him with a smile.

"Don't apologise. I didn't mean to disappear. I think I just got scared."

"Why?"

"While I was talking to you, while you were talking to me, I felt I was getting closer to myself. You looked at me and you seemed to see me. To see me, not the characters I'd invented. But then you said that thing, and it was as if you weren't talking to me, but to one of those characters. The ground disappeared from under me. I shut my eyes so as not to fall and when I opened them again I was standing in front of a cow."

"You saw the cows, too?"

"Yes, they're around, but let's not talk about cows."

"Let's not talk about cows," the engineer of bridges agreed. "Who else did you meet?"

"I wanted to meet you. To meet you again. But I only got other people. I asked everybody about you."

"Did you meet anyone who remembered me?"

"Yes. A sailor. He said you were going to help me to cross the river."

"And you believed him?"

"I've been practising that, believing. What do you say, shall we build a bridge, or a raft?"

"I've learned how to build bridges."

"So let's do it! I'd also prefer to build a bridge. That would work for us and for other people, too."

"And the shade?"

"There's so much light, and all you see is the shade?"

She gave him her hand and pulled him towards her. The man saw a path shimmering through the elephant-grass. The river *approaching. He turned. Behind them, the mulemba was rising up to a vast height. Thousands of birds in every colour were flying free of its dense branches, their wings disordering the brilliant blue of the sky. The woman's hand was hot and soft, and everything was beginning again.*

9

Cornelia is asleep, stretched out on a sun lounger, on the huge terrace adjoining her room. She is dreaming about snakes. She sees herself lying on a bed with tall legs, in the middle of a very green savanna, under a sky that is hard and bright as steel. Dozens of snakes are surrounding the bed. They come closer, hissing, talking to one another in mysterious whistled languages. The largest of them, as big as a construction crane, fixes its eyes on hers, but instead of a whistle, what comes out of its mouth is that delightful little iPhone sound announcing the arrival of a new message. The writer opens her eyes. She picks up her phone, which she had left on the floor beside her chair. The screen is lit up, and she reads:

"Did you hear the news? They've closed the airports. They say they're cutting off the internet. People are panicking. There are queues to get out of the city. I don't know where they're going. But you, where you are, at the end of the world there, you're definitely safe. Only people at the ends of the world are safe. Don't be scared for me. Whatever happens, I'll get to you. I'm going to die in Africa, in your arms, many years from now. I love you, life of mine."

Pierre had sent the message five days earlier.

Cornelia gets up. Her legs are trembling, her heart out of time, beating just beneath her skin. The streetlamps are lit up. The sound of laughter, applause, the rise of a chanting whose meaning she can only just understand: "The power's back!"

She puts on her hotel robe and leaves the room. She finds Jude on the veranda, leaning out over the street. She calls:

"Jude!"

He turns.

"Yeah?"

"I got a message." She holds out her phone. "What's happened?"

Jude reads.

"I don't understand. I'll put mine to charge."

In the hallway he meets Luzia, who throws herself into his arms. She's sweaty, nervous, tripping over her words.

"I ran all the way. Have you heard what's happened?"

"What's happened?"

"Somebody's set off a nuclear bomb!"

THE SIXTH DAY

That year, the rain rained so much that memory lost all its meaning. Throats became blocked up with slime and the foreheads that the old people rested on their hands merged with their fingers and their arms with their legs and graceful gestures merged bodies and young children became glued to their mothers' breasts. Only mouths insisted on remaining open and when later the rain ended, out of those mouths came big black birds that quickly flew away from those places.

RUY DUARTE DE CARVALHO, *Sign*

I

It was two minutes after midnight. The internet had arrived like a powerful gale, dragging with it a hailstorm of messages, all of them written five days earlier, and then disappeared again. Daniel, who had been woken by the children chanting in the street, celebrating the return of the electricity, came down from the terrace, plugged in his phone, and soon he was sitting on the kitchen floor, puzzled, reading fifty-two new messages, most of them reporting that a nuclear bomb had exploded. The information all disagreed. It was Iran, some claimed. The Americans are getting ready to bomb Tehran. Russia is threatening to bomb the United States if they bomb Iran. It wasn't Iran but Russia, others were saying. More than thirty thousand people had died. A hundred thousand wounded. Demonstrators occupy and destroy Iran's embassy in London. Millions of people in panic quit New York, Washington DC, Los Angeles, Miami and other major US cities, creating endless traffic queues. It wasn't Iran, nor Russia. Maybe radical Islamists supported by Saudi Arabia, with technology supplied by the Russian mafia. In Rio de Janeiro and São Paulo, thousands of people pray in the squares, doing penance and awaiting the Rapture. There is looting in many European cities. General chaos.

Daniel gets up, dizzy. Moira is standing in front of him, very serious, the baby tied to her back with a kapulana, a telephone in her right hand.

"Looks like the world really has ended after all."

"Have you tried calling anyone?"

"I tried talking to a friend, she's in New York. The phones aren't working. Incidentally, the internet has gone down again. At least we've still got electricity."

"What do we do?"

"Let's go to the Terraço das Quitandas. They must all be there."

"At this time?! And the baby?"

"The baby can come with us. She's an angel, she's sleeping."

2

Moira was correct: the writers were spread across the hotel's big tearoom, the veranda and the main terrace, talking to one another, sharing messages from their phones, swapping news and rumours. Uli sees the couple approaching him. He's holding a bottle of beer. Daniel looks at him, surprised:

"You, drinking beer? I've never seen you drink anything alcoholic before."

"This is a good day for first times."

"The end of the world, you mean?"

"Is there any more news?" asks Moira.

"It's all five days old. We don't know what's happened since."

Jude and Luzia are talking in one corner of the patio, far from the other writers. The Nigerian is complaining about the electric light, which he now finds too bright and crude, stealing the city's soul. Luzia accuses him, teasing, of romanticising poverty, the way rich tourists from northern countries do when visiting African villages. Jude doesn't defend himself. Yes, he admits, he does sometimes look at the continent from outside, with all the fears and prejudices of a common British citizen. Luzia is surprised.

"Is that true?"

"It is. I'm Nigerian and I'm English. I'm not sure that's an altogether peaceable combination. Sometimes it feels like a dissonant mix. Or even worse, a colonial process, with my British ego charging on horseback against my Nigerian ego and cutting off its head. There are days I find myself a foreigner to myself."

Luzia doesn't know what to say. The laughter of the others reaches them in pieces, slightly sad, like bottles abandoned on the floor after a big party. The young woman presses her body up against the novelist's. She whispers in his ear:

"And what now?"

Jude put his arms around her waist. They kiss. Luzia unbuttons her shirt and presses her bare breasts against his chest. He shuts his eyes and sees himself, an eight-year-old boy, one Sunday morning, on Calabar beach, being dragged away by a gigantic wave, while his mother rushes over to rescue him.

3

Juvêncio sees the sun come up, from the terrace of his house, without realising that it is the first morning of the world. At eight o'clock, already at the station, he manages to persuade Ali Habib to cross the bridge, but only after promising to take him to dinner at Feitoria, that same night, a place the sergeant had been wanting to go for a long time but which, on his own meagre salary, he would never be able to afford.

"And what about the spirits?" asks Habib, when they've already gone two kilometres.

None of the other officers had agreed to go with them. The early morning sun is casting quick flashes onto the sea, which is smooth and very calm, though murky, filled with mud, with leaves, rags, disposable nappies, plastic bags and bottles and a thousand other useless objects, the leftovers of a world erased by the storm. The two men see the swollen carcass of a donkey float past, a mob of crows arguing over it, shrieking loudly.

"What spirits?" asks Juvêncio, irritated.

"Those voices . . ."

"Are you hearing voices? Human voices?"

The sergeant shrinks back. Oh no, not yet, just the crows, but who knew what they'd find on the other side, a chasm, a black cloud, a vast desert in flames, with a legion of damned souls clamouring for revenge. Juvêncio quickens his pace. The other man runs after him. The mainland is already in view: the red hill, with broken-up pockets of green; walls that rise up from the water like desperate hands of the drowned. The road has vanished. The gate at which guards monitored the coming and going of vehicles is planted in the mud, all twisted, like a piece of wire that a bored giant had been using to play with. Nobody is there to meet them – no shipwrecks, no demons. The police chief doesn't stop. He sinks his boots into the mud and keeps going. Habib hesitates:

"Boss, there's no-one in sight . . ."

"They probably evacuated the population to Nacala or Nampula. Let's see if there's anyone who needs our help."

There are dhows stuck in the grasses, five hundred metres from the sea. All the houses have been destroyed. The fallen trees obstruct the two men's passage even more, Juvêncio's shirt is soaked in sweat, his breathing is heavy, his face swollen from the effort. Habib is secretly praying, asking Allah, the merciful, the compassionate, to please place a hole in the chief's path so that the man might trip and twist an ankle and they can finally stop and rest. God ignores him. They continue in silence for over an hour. Then suddenly a clearing opens up and, rising before them, intact and serene, absolutely identical to the day it first opened, almost a century earlier, they see the small Lumbo aerodrome. In the middle of the runway there is an old man, sitting on a chair, with a Hasselblad resting in his lap.

Ali Habib stops short, very rigid.

"A demon!"

Juvêncio laughs.

"No, a man of flesh and bone! In this case, rather more bone than flesh, but still just like you and me, sitting in a chair, in the sun."

"How's that possible?! Nobody was left in the world . . ."

"We're about to find out."

As they approach, the old man gets up and takes a series of photographs of them. Finally, he holds out his hand. He speaks a hesitant Portuguese, with a strong French accent:

"Hello! I'm Charles-Maurice, photographer."

Juvêncio shakes his hand. The old man seems very weak, his dark skin all wrinkled, his very white, frizzy hair pulled back. But he has big, strong fingers and a firm wrist. His bluish eyes hold the policeman's, infinitely calm and ironic.

"What are you doing here?" asks Juvêncio.

"I'm dying."

"What?!"

"I'm dying, Mister Policeman. I've come here to die. It's an occupation that takes up all my time."

He invites them into the aerodrome's departure lounge, a very clean, very tidy place, leads them to the small bar and serves them tea. He tells them that it was there, in that aerodrome, that his career as a photographer began. He was fifteen and he had travelled to Mozambique in the company of his father, a French aristocrat who had fallen in love with a Senegalese nurse, in Paris, and who, following her death in a car accident, had decided to spend the rest of his life travelling the world. They had been residing in Lumbo's Grande Hotel for five months when they learned that Rita Hayworth, the great Hollywood star, would be disembarking in that small town the very next morning, accompanying her husband, Ali Aga Khan, on a visit to the Ismaili community. Charles-Maurice stole his father's Kodak and positioned himself next to the runway waiting for the plane to land. Nobody suspected the mixed-race boy with the small rucksack slung over his shoulder, who sneaked in between the police officers and bodyguards, got himself into the waiting room, shouted the actress's name, photographed her and ran off.

"I thought my father would be furious, but he laughed a great deal when he heard about it. I think he was proud of my initiative. He bought me a good camera, a tripod and developing gear, and encouraged me to photograph all the cities we passed through. I followed his advice. When my father died, four years later, in Manila, I discovered he had left me little more than a few family jewels, along with a vineyard in Provence. He had squandered his fortune at the poker tables."

Charles-Maurice sold the jewels and the vineyard and settled in Paris. He showed the photos he'd taken over the previous four years to the editor-in-chief of a big French magazine: pictures of carnival in Cape Town; Herero women in Namibia, in their Victorian-inspired dresses, watching a movie in an open-air cinema; men dancing tango together, in a Buenos Aires bar; bathers on Iracema beach, in Fortaleza, gathered around the inflated cadaver of a whale. The journalist studied the photos, with growing amazement.

"And you're how old?"

Charles-Maurice worked for that magazine for fifty-six years. He got used to seeing the world through the lens of a camera. After he retired, at the turn of the century, he decided to devote himself to reading the thousands of novels he'd been buying, on his countless work trips, from bookshops on five continents. The news that a nuclear bomb had exploded surprised him in his flat, in Paris, while he was rereading Italo Calvino's *Marcovaldo*, in its original language, lying in a hammock he'd bought in Manaus. One week earlier, a doctor had diagnosed him with a brain tumour. Without a second thought, the old photographer bought a ticket for a flight that was due to leave four hours later, bound for Johannesburg, gathered some clothes into a small suitcase and called a cab. In Joburg, he boarded another flight to Nampula, on an almost empty flight that had trouble landing due to the heavy rain. The first taxi driver he approached refused to take him to Lumbo:

"There's a cyclone to the north, coming down to Ilha de Moçambique. They're evacuating the whole population. This trip is insane."

The second driver, a peaceful giant, with the solid, smooth body of a seal, and a similar oceanic sadness, listened to him without any sign of fear or amazement.

"Lumbo? Let's go."

"And what about the cyclone?"

"So you don't want to go?"

"I do."

"Well, then – let's go."

It was only at the entrance to the tiny town, after they'd passed about ten buses headed in the opposite direction, escorted by military lorries, that Charles-Maurice mentioned the name of Lumbo's Grande Hotel.

"The Grande Hotel?" the driver was surprised. "You're sure?"

The man drove him through the lightning-flashes to some tall, solemn ruins, in which the photographer recognised the building where he had been happy. He would await death leaning up against those old walls. It was the cab driver who dissuaded him:

"There's not a single room left with a roof, senhor."

"And what about the aerodrome?"

"Oh, the aerodrome was restored not long ago. It's as good as new."

"Excellent. That is my destination."

"It's not in operation, senhor. There's nobody there."

"That's not a problem."

The driver left him at the aerodrome, sheltered from the rain on the broad covered veranda that surrounds the building. Charles-Maurice remained in a chair for some time, watching the beginning of the end of the world. Bored at the beginning of that ending, which was much less dramatic than he'd imagined, he got up and tried to open one of the doors. It was locked. He tried the others, without any hope, and then one of them opened, like a portal in time, dragging him into the same room where, exactly eighty years ago, he had photographed Rita Hayworth. Startled, he once again smelled the great American star's perfume at the moment when she, noticing the camera, had raised her hands, trying to hide her face. He heard, once again, the shout from Ali Aga Khan – "Get him!" – while a powerful discharge of adrenaline flooded his brain. He saw his life unfolding, one click after another, realising for the first time, with a hopeless clarity, the clever illusion that is the passage of time and the uselessness that is the meaning of being alive. Nonetheless, he had been happy.

"And you stayed here throughout the whole storm, senhor?" asks Juvêncio.

"Ever since I arrived in Lumbo, yes. Waiting for the world to explode into thousands of gigantic atomic mushrooms."

"Alone?"

"I'm not sure."

"You're not sure?"

"I think I heard voices, but I never saw anyone . . ."

"The spirits!" whispers Ali Habib. "He heard the spirits."

Juvêncio silences the sergeant with a glare, which does not go unnoticed by the French photographer.

"Perhaps spirits, perhaps hallucinations produced by a sick mind," says Charles-Maurice. "In any case, they brought me mangoes."

"Mangoes?"

"Mangoes. Oranges. Avocadoes. I've survived on fruit and biscuits. The biscuits I found here, in the kitchen of the bar. As well as the teabags. I've also used a gas stove."

"You have occupied a public building, senhor. That cannot be."

"I am so sorry. I must crave your forgiveness."

"Very well. Given the situation, it's best to stay here. I will ask them to deliver you some provisions. I just don't understand why this building was saved. The storm devastated the whole city."

"I went out a few times to take photographs. I saw the wind carrying off boats. It looked like a living thing. A wild animal, racing through the streets, shaking the houses, tearing up large trees by the roots. Fortunately, it never came close to the aerodrome. Here, it just rained."

Juvêncio and Ali Habib say goodbye to the man, who sits back down on the chair, in the sun, much older all of a sudden, and they return to the bridge. Next to the place where the Jembesse fish market used to be, they find two boys digging in the mud with shovels. The chief of police recognises them. They are his neighbours.

"What are you doing there?"

One of the boys puts down his shovel and looks at them, defiantly.

"We're excavating the country, chief."

"Good luck!" Juvêncio laughs. "You'll have to dig for the rest of your lives."

4

Júlio Zivane sees Ofélia going down the steps and into the sea. He takes a deep breath and follows her. Fortunately the tide is so low that even there, at the furthest end of the jetty, he can touch the sand. He takes a couple of strokes with his arms, without much conviction, and immediately swims right back to the steps. Ofélia joins him.

"Are you scared of the sea?"

"I am. Very scared. I'm like Uli in that respect."

"Uli won't even come into the sea. It makes no sense being scared. Not of the sea, nor of anything. Not now, when we're all already dead, or almost dead."

"Still, I am afraid."

"You know what we should do, the two of us?"

"Have a kid?"

"That's a bit late for me. A bit late for the world. But we could write a book together."

Zivane climbs the stairs to the wooden platform. He takes a pair of towels out of a small straw basket and holds one out to the Angolan writer. He dries himself off with the other. A four-hands book? He likes the idea.

"A novel?"

"Of course, a novel. I mostly write poetry, but I do venture into fiction, too."

"A novel demands a lot of time. Why would we start writing a novel when everything's coming to an end?"

"We should always write as if everything was coming to an end."

"So that everything doesn't?"

"Yes, so that it doesn't."

"And for whom?"

"For those who will restart the world."

"When do we begin?"

"Right now, every minute counts."

They both sit down on the deck. From the little straw basket Ofélia pulls out a pen with black ink and a small red-covered notebook, her "Dream trash", where she jots down phrases and ideas. She opens it. She says that she dreamed about a woman lying on a mat, suffering from a bout of malaria. When she woke up, she wrote a poem. She reads:

It happened on a Saturday:
stretched out on a charpai,
burning with fever, Ofélia had a revelation:
she saw that the Island was a veranda over God,
and thought this inevitable:
like the existence of the atheist sky.

Júlio Zivane asks her to read it again.

"It's beautiful," he says. He thinks a little: "Why Ofélia? Is it you?"

"Course not. After this one, I wrote a whole series of others in a single burst. They tell the story of this woman, Ofélia, who lives here, on Ilha de Moçambique, and who is going to be the mother of a little boy but doesn't know it yet. In my poem, there's no distinction between past, present and future. Everything happens on the same plane."

"Read me another."

Ofélia hesitates. She leafs through the notebook. Finally, she reads:

The island is a comma in the sea of time.
Ofélia arrived home in a daze one evening:
"I've found God!" she said, as she opened her hand.
And I saw a little bird with a broken wing.
"It's just a bird!" I said.
But it was clearly God.

Zivane gets excited. He likes the idea of making no distinction between timeframes, though he finds it hard to imagine how they might sustain this over a whole novel. Ofélia says it's best not to think about the book's architecture. It's got to be the story that chooses the shape. They should let the characters run free, on the loose, let them find the best paths.

"And the narrator?" asks Zivane. "Who's the narrator?"

"I don't know," admits Ofélia. "I have no idea. Maybe her son, before he's even been conceived, seeing everything from somewhere in the future."

"Before existing, he's already in the future?"

"Exactly. The characters are in all times simultaneously."

"Right. And the father? Who's the father?"

"You could be the father."

"Me?!"

"Yes, you. Júlio Zivane. Mozambican writer, hair dealer. You're very much in love with each other, you and this Ofélia, but you cannot live together."

"Why not?"

"Are you married?"

"No, no!"

Ofélia laughs.

"I already knew you weren't. I made enquiries."

"Seriously?"

"Seriously. I asked Uli. I know you used to be married."

"Yes. I have a daughter, in Maputo. I don't see her much."

"Why did you separate?"

"I drank a lot. I was a confused person, and in real distress."

"You were?"

"The last three or four days I've been a different man. I've stopped drinking. I feel much calmer, more lucid."

"Because you've spent four days without drinking?"

"No. Because I took the decision not to go back to drinking. I'm sure I won't drink again."

"That's the advantage of stopping drinking right before the end of the world. On the other hand, maybe we'd be happier drinking. Celebrating the end."

"Even when I was a confused and distressed man, I liked life. I don't celebrate the end of life."

"You're right. Let's get back to our novel. The character inspired by you is in love with Ofélia. And she with him. Júlio, our character, drinks a lot. He started drinking years earlier, to fight his shyness. His tongue only loosens up after a glass or two. When he's drunk, he becomes rather amusing. People like him. When he arrives home, however, his joy turns to bitterness. Ofélia feels like she's living with two different men."

"And she doesn't like that?"

"No, she's a fierce defender of monogamy."

"I thought she was a free woman."

"She's a free woman, who believes in monogamy."

"I understand. So, they fall in love, but they can't live together. Until one day, that fragmented man – Júlio, right? – he meets his father. The father who's been dead a long time. And his father shows him a book and in that book is his whole life, past and future, in countless versions, what he was and what he could have been, what he will become if he follows one path or another. And his father says to him: 'Son, all the choices are yours.'"

"Free will, God's great swindle. And what do you think Júlio chooses?"

"Júlio chooses to be Ofélia's only man."

"And do they stay together forever, Júlio and Ofélia?"

"There's no way of knowing that."

"Why not?"

"It's an open ending. I like open endings."

"Me, too, mainly because if it's open it can't be the end. Shall we write?"

Júlio Zivane takes the notebook from her and puts it back

into the straw basket. He gets up and holds out his hand to his fellow writer.

"On such a lovely day, Ofélia? Let's take our story for a walk."

5

Daniel is at home, changing Tetembua's nappy, when the phone rings, startling him. He puts the baby down in her cot and answers. It's Uli. His friend tells him what is obvious, that telephone connections have been re-established. He adds that he's managed to speak to his wife, Doralice, in Maputo. The world had lived through five days of extreme nervousness. It had been learned, in the meantime, that the explosion might in fact have been not the result of a terrorist attack but simply a terrible accident. Though many remained unconvinced, this official explanation was at least enough to drain away the tension between the different powers. The prospect of a nuclear war, however, had given people a wake-up call. Huge spontaneous demonstrations happened in all the big cities of the world, from New York to Moscow, via Delhi and Beijing, demanding the complete dismantling of the different nuclear arsenals. The mood of panic had given way to a festive insurgency, with people dancing and singing, as they burned dolls with the faces of political leaders. "It's a huge party!" had been Doralice's summary. "Even here, in Maputo, there are people on the streets. I think humanity's being reborn."

Daniel puts down the phone. He remembers the reusable

nappy, washes it, and puts it out to dry on the patio. Only then does he sit down to read the dozens of messages that he's receiving from all over. The phone rings again and this time it's Moira, who is very agitated, repeating to him what he already knows, that the world almost ended and that humanity is now out in the squares of every city, dancing, when really it would be much better if they were gathered into the appropriate forums, discussing policies to prevent future apocalypses, resulting, for example, from global warming. Tetembua starts to cry. Daniel says goodbye to his wife and goes to fetch the baby from the cot. He goes out with her onto the street, and only then does the little girl fall quiet. There are people walking, in a hurry. Two youths on the corner are speaking on their phones. Commander Juvêncio goes past, almost at a run, followed by two police officers. The writer stops him in his tracks.

"Commander! Have you heard the news?"

Juvêncio stops.

"Of course. Who hasn't heard?" His eyes don't come to rest on Daniel, but continue to follow the movement of the people. Children give festive yells. At the end of the road, a group of women is approaching, clapping and singing. Finally the commander looks at Daniel. "I was on the mainland this morning. All destroyed. We saw nobody, apart from a French tourist, very old. And now they tell me there are people crossing the bridge. I'm headed that way, to try to figure out where these people are coming from."

Juvêncio walks off, fast and firm, followed by his two officers. Daniel continues as far as the Âncora d'Ouro, with the baby in his arms, her eyes wide open, alert to life. Luzia and Jude are sitting at one of the tables. They are kissing, oblivious to the noise around them. Then they notice the Angolan and laugh.

"Have a seat," says Jude. "Tell us what you know."

Daniel sits down.

"Same as you, I imagine."

Luzia takes the girl from his arms and rocks her.

"So beautiful, this one! To think that the world almost ended, and here we were, totally unaware of it, writing and discussing literature."

"The islands are reliquaries," says Daniel. "After the world's ended, it'll restart on the islands."

6

The movement on the bridge is intense. Juvêncio is standing there, beside the sentry box, watching the people who are arriving from the mainland on foot, by bicycle and by motorbike, transporting live chickens, tied by the legs, bags of fruit and vegetables. Suddenly he jumps right in front of one of the bicycles. The guy riding it stops just centimetres from him. He has sad, startled eyes, which avoid the police chief's, not like somebody who feels guilty but like somebody who is used to being blamed.

"And you've come from where?"

"From Land, boss."

Juvêncio smiles at this answer. He knows where Land is, it's a small village in the interior, far from the main roads.

"And did it rain a lot there?"

"Yes, boss, a lot. But not like Lumbo or Mossuril. It was normal rain."

"And what have you come to do on the island?"

"I left my wife sick in the hospital. I tried coming sooner but there was no way. From Namialo onwards there was no road left. Nothing at all."

"What do you mean, nothing?"

"Only that water that erased people. A lot of people got erased."

"They died?"

"It wasn't death, boss. The water came and erased them."

Juvêncio senses Ali Habib behind him shudder. He hears him moan.

"It's like I told you, commander, that rain, it wasn't rain."

The man from the country asks permission to continue on his way. Juvêncio steps aside and he goes. Ali Habib sees the furious look in his chief's eyes and regrets having spoken. Now, however, it's too late. He goes on, in a frightened voice.

"It's sorcerers' work, commander."

"Oh it is, is it? In that case, do tell me, my dear Habib: if that magical water erased all the houses, the trees, the animals and the people, where has the world come bursting back from?"

Ali Habib takes off his képi and scratches his head. He makes an effort to keep his voice firm.

"Senhor, you should know that not everything has been un-erased. Most of the people who were erased haven't come back yet. And also the un-erased places aren't the same . . ."

"What do you mean, they aren't the same?"

"Apparently they're different."

"But different how?"

"The houses look the same, but their owners feel like foreigners in them. They sleep, and they dream other people's dreams. And the people, the un-erased ones, come back as if they were the same, they look the same, only with memories that don't belong to them."

"How can you know the memories don't belong to them?"

"Boss, my brother-in-law knows one of the un-erased. He came home this morning, remembering things he couldn't possibly have known."

"Why?"

"Because they're things that happened to his grandchildren. And he doesn't even have kids yet."

7

Sitting in the small bar of the art gallery of the Hotel Villa Sands, Cornelia looks at the girl standing in front of her, feeling like she's repeating the same moment for a second time. She calls the waitress over to her table and asks for two croissants, then offers one to the girl. The child hesitates a moment, works up the courage, takes two steps forward and picks it up. The writer tries hard to remember her name, something Arabic, she's sure of that, something to do with the moon or moonlight.

"Ainur, have a seat here." She gestures towards the free chair. "Come on, sweetie, sit with me. I'll order a soft drink for you."

The girl sits down, very upright in the chair, her tall round hairdo illuminating the gloom. She gives a nod and smiles, as if she understood English. Looking up, the writer sees a huge man, standing beneath the broad stone archway that links the patio to the gallery.

"Pierre?!"

Pierre Mpanzu Kanda, who has watched the whole scene in silence, runs over to the woman, wraps his arms around her and pulls her into an improvised kind of dance, laughing happily. Cornelia laughs, too. Ainur imitates them. She claps happily, singing a song in Makua.

Pierre decided to travel to Mozambique as soon as the US reopened its airspace. It hadn't been easy to get there. Owing to the cyclone, there had been no commercial flights to Mozambique. Finally he'd managed to get a plane chartered by the Red Cross to bring him from Johannesburg to Nacala.

That night, Cornelia started to write a novel about an albino girl, Ainur, who was given by her parents when still a baby to a north American missionary couple, so that they might take her far away from Africa. Thirty years later, Ainur returns to Tanzania, the country of her birth, intending to film a documentary about the persecution of albinos. The novel will not have as many readers as the previous one, *The Woman Who Was a Cockroach*, but it will win the Booker. Ainur, the Makua girl, will never read it.

8

Night is falling when Ali Habib jumps off the motorbike at the Lumbo aerodrome. Goia, the young, lanky moto-taxi driver, glances quickly at his watch.

"Forty-nine minutes, boss. Nobody could get here this fast, not like this, driving through the scrubland, in the middle of all the debris and the mud."

The police officer agrees and thanks him, then asks him to wait a little. He's just going to drop off a bag of cassava flour and three fat slices of fresh tuna to the old French tourist, on Juvêncio's instructions. Then he'll go back to the island. He doesn't want to stay too long on the mainland. He distrusts that ground, still soaked with the prodigious water that for days had erased the world. He goes up to the veranda and claps his hands loudly, but nobody answers him. He shouts:

"Senhor! Senhor Carlos-Maurício!"

Nobody answers. Ali Habib looks through the window and sees the shape of Charles-Maurice in the small bar, sitting, rigid, with his head slumped onto one of the tables. The policeman can tell there's no point calling out to him. He phones Juvêncio:

"Boss, the old man's died."

One hour later, Juvêncio arrives, on another moto-taxi, sweating copiously and cursing his bad luck. Just now when everything seemed like it was about to get back to normal, a Frenchman had to go and die on him? Before leaving the station, he phoned the French embassy in Maputo. They told him an embassy employee would be there the following morning, accompanied by a doctor, to ascertain Charles-Maurice's cause of death, which they presumed was natural, owing to the man's advanced age, and to deal with repatriating the body to France. In the meantime they asked him to ensure the integrity of the corpse and of the traveller's belongings.

"We'll spend the night here," Juvêncio announces to his sergeant.

Ali Habib looks at him, appalled.

"Me, too?!"

"You, too. That way we can take turns. You sleep a bit, then I'll sleep afterwards."

"No, boss, please, not that. You promised, chief, you said you'd take me to dinner at Feitoria."

Juvêncio shrugs.

"Sorry about that, sergeant. We'll go tomorrow."

Ali Habib looks like a child about to collapse into uncontrollable sobs.

"Please, commander sir, this place is bewitched."

"Nonsense!"

"Just look around, boss. It's like they opened the place today. Lumbo's practically disappeared, but the cyclone didn't even touch this spot. Not even a broken window . . ."

Juvêncio ignores him.

"Is the door open? How did you get in?"

"Get in?! I didn't go in."

"You didn't go in?" Juvêncio tries to control his irritation. "So how do you know the man's dead? Maybe he's just sleeping."

"He's dead. He's not moving."

The commander turns the door handle and enters the building. The air is hot and it smells bad, but it's not yet the heavy stink of death, which Juvêncio knows well. The old man can't have died too many hours ago. He has his camera on his lap and he is holding it with both hands. His face is resting on its side on the table, eyes open, lips forming a happy smile.

"Come inside!" Juvêncio yells to Ali Habib.

The sergeant comes in fearfully, looking all around him.

The commander asks him to help photograph the corpse. Together, they lay the body out on the floorboards. It's not yet rigid. Juvêncio closes the eyelids. Ali Habib stands up, trembling.

"I'm just going to wash my hands."

He moves towards the bathroom. Moments later, he's back, very agitated.

"Boss! In the bathroom! You got to take a look . . ."

Juvêncio goes with him. The Frenchman had transformed the place into a photo darkroom. A ghostly red light reveals the containers of chemicals for developing and fixing, along with an old enlarger. The commander counts twenty-five pictures hanging from a line, with clothes pegs, drying. In one of them, he recognises the grinning face of the Nigerian writer who'd been at the station, with Moira. What was the guy's name? Júlio. No, Júlio was the Mozambican. Jude. Yes, Jude, he's quite sure. Another photo shows that strange woman, who was also Nigerian, the one who'd come across the bridge. There are various others he can't identify. The photos were taken right there, in the bar of the aerodrome, probably just hours earlier. What could have happened here?

He returns to the bar and puts some water in a teapot. He lights the stove. Minutes later, he pours himself some tea. The sergeant is lying on the floor, next to Charles-Maurice's corpse, and he is snoring. A gust of wind makes the window-panes shudder. Juvêncio Baptista Nguane thinks about his grandmother, old Rainata, interpreter of dreams and of breezes and of all the pantings and babblings of nature. She would have an explanation for everything that has happened these past few days. Personally, he would rather not know.

THE SEVENTH DAY

Alone, amid the intense astonishment, I rejoice.
The blue sky, the patio ablaze beneath the sun.
I will never hear the crickets sing again.

OFÉLIA EASTERMANN, *Awaiting the End of the World*

I

Daniel is in his study, finishing a column for an Angolan weekly entitled "Everything eternal is soon over", when he hears someone at the front door. Three loud knocks. He gets up and goes to open it. The tall, robust old man, who Luzia claims is Pedro Calunga Nzagi, smiles at him. He holds out his solid giant's hand.

"Hello! May I come in?"

The writer steps aside to let the man past. He invites him to sit in one of the wicker chairs, in the living room, and chooses another for himself, from where he has a view of the yard. His heart is pounding. He finds it hard to swallow. The sun, which is flooding the yard and coming in through the kitchen's large, open windows, shining on the red ochre living-room floor, calms him a little. The old man opens a leather folder and pulls out a fat black notebook, which he places in Daniel's hands.

"They asked me to give you this. It's a manuscript, a kind of novel . . ."

"Who's the author?"

"Pedro Calunga Nzagi."

"And is that not you, senhor?"

The man smiles.

"Apologies for not having introduced myself as I should. My name is Jorge Bueno and I'm a general in the reserves of the Angolan armed forces. I know who you are, senhor, of course, I've read many of your reports. I've also read your books. As a reader, I'm sorry you've given up journalism."

"And besides being Jorge Bueno, senhor, are you also Pedro Nzagi?"

"What does that matter?"

"It does matter, it seems to me."

"Oh, no, it doesn't. Not in the least."

Daniel notices that his fingers are shaking. He puts the manuscript down on a low table, which is piled with books and magazines, and folds his arms. He doesn't want the other man to notice his nerves.

"What am I supposed to do with the manuscript?"

"Read it, please."

"And then?"

"Then do whatever you think best."

Jorge Bueno says this and gets up. Daniel seems to feel the room shrinking, the rarefied air burning his lungs. The general holds out his hand.

"I've got a cab waiting."

He takes three steps towards the door, opens it, and goes out onto the street. He gets into a car. He says goodbye with a slight nod. Daniel watches him go, unable to utter a single word, then shuts the door, sits down and opens the notebook. On the first page he reads, in black ink, in clear, firm handwriting:

The Benchimol Enigma
A novel by Pedro Calunga Nzagi

Daniel laughs out loud.

"What the fuck?!"

He turns the page and starts to read.

"The boy was born, 2.8 kilos, at the Benguela Railroad clinic, in Huambo. A still night. A vast moon, very round and red, shining in the sky. His father, Ernesto Benchimol, employed with the Benguela Railroad, would never forget that moon."

Daniel skips ahead a few pages. He reads:

"He was the youngest. His older brothers teased him, tirelessly, for being the thinnest, the most delicate, the most fearful. Ernesto trained swimmers at the Railroad Club pool. He was obsessed with making his sons into champions. The youngest disappointed him. He never won a medal. But the criticisms and defeats, rather than traumatising him, strengthened him. Daniel became immune to gossip and ridicule."

The book sets out episodes from his childhood that he has never told anybody. He reads, with shame, the story of how, aged nine years, ten months and five days, he killed a cat with a shot from an air rifle. A few pages on, Pedro Calunga Nzagi, or the Devil in his name, gives a very detailed description of the afternoon when the young Daniel Benchimol, having climbed to the highest branch of the big avocado tree that his maternal grandmother had planted in the yard, saw the young woman who lived next-door naked, bathed in sunlight. From there he could also see his older brother, Samuel, masturbating behind the wall.

Daniel turns the pages furiously, fearfully. He hastens past the sad days of his marriage to Lucrécia, the fights and reconciliations, attends the birth of his first child, Karinguiri, sees her take her first steps, skip rope, sing in the mysterious language she invented to speak to the birds, before she was even able to say thirty words in Portuguese. He cries, without realising it, as he ages, his hair still strong but ever whiter, witnessing upheavals, wars, small lessons in heroism and unpredictable generosity. The best and worst of humanity. He meets Moira, certain he's seen her before, somewhere in the future. He quits journalism and moves to Ilha de Moçambique. Tetembua is born. A stranger comes into his house to deliver a manuscript. He accompanies his younger daughter to school. They play by the sea. He argues with Moira, one convulsed evening, on discovering that for some years she'd been keeping up an affair with Uli. His wife is bitten by a dragon-fish, while swimming beside the coast, and almost dies.

Daniel shuts the book and returns to the present. He goes out onto the patio. On the cement slab that covers the water-tank, there is a metal tub containing some damp clothes. He tosses the clothes onto the grass, and puts the exercise book inside. In the kitchen, under the sink, he finds a can of petrol. He takes that and a box of matches and returns to the patio. He sprinkles the notebook with the fuel and throws in a lit match. He sits on the slab, the tub at his feet, watching the rapid conflagration of his life. He runs his fingers through the flame and barely feels it.

"What are you doing?"

It's Moira. She is walking over, carrying the little girl on her back, tied with a kapulana. Daniel is startled.

"Nothing. I'm burning some old papers."

The woman comes closer, intrigued. She turns over the ashes with a stick, and pulls out the last page of the notebook, which has not yet been completely consumed by the fire, and reads the last line:

Ilha de Moçambique, 30 November 2019.

"That's today's date! Old papers?!"

"Just some notes."

"You're looking pale. And your hands are shaking. Don't you want to tell me the truth?"

"The truth?" Daniel looks at his wife, with big frightened eyes. "And does that even exist?"

Moira takes the little girl off her back and lays her down on the grass, on the kapulana, in the shade of the lemon tree. Tetembua smiles, amazed, to see the sun's rays dancing between its leaves. Her mother looks affectionately at her, then hugs her husband.

"What is it that's scared you so much?"

Daniel takes a deep breath.

"What am I?"

"What do you think you are?"

"An invention . . ."

"And aren't we all?"

Moira holds the back of his neck with both hands and kisses him on the lips. Daniel feels the heat being unleashed into his fictitious body, a true blaze, that expands through his flesh and stiffens it. His wife gives him a shove.

"Hey, don't get too excited . . ."

She picks up the girl and disappears into the house.

Daniel lies down in the sun, on the blazing hot slab. He feels the light burning his face. He sees birds scratching lines across the blue. He smiles.

He *is* alive, whether he's alive or not.

217

2

When Dona Cinema turned ninety, her children decided to take her for a doctor's appointment. It was the first and last time she ever went into a hospital. In the opinion of the nurse who saw her, the old lady was so scrawny that death simply had no way of functioning inside her. "She is never going to die," he pronounced solemnly, "she has mummified in life."

Dona Cinema had been a dressmaker. After retirement, her sole occupation had been telling stories. One day, a journalist from Maputo appeared on the island. Somebody invited him for a drink in Dona Sara Amade's yard. A month later, the man had been forgotten, until Dona Francisca de Bragança received a newspaper carrying a report whose first line read "Dona Sara Amade is cinema for the poor". And thus she came to be called Dona Cinema.

Uli is sitting in the hotel bar, drinking a Coke, when he receives a message from the journalist who, fifteen years earlier, had interviewed Dona Cinema. They were close friends.

"I heard you were on the island. You've got to meet this amazing character, a great storyteller, old Sara Amade."

With a wave, the writer calls Abdul over.

"Abdul, do you know a lady called Sara Amade?"

"Dona Cinema, yes, she's my grandmother."

"Dona Cinema? Your grandmother? Your father's mother?"

"My mother's mother."

"I hear she tells stories."

"There are stories today, over in her yard."

"Can I go?"

"Anyone can go. You just got to take some money for the drinks."

Uli waits at the bar until Abdul has finished his shift. They leave together. First they make their way along the paved streets of the stone city, and then, guided by the moonlight, across the dusty labyrinth that is the interior of the macuti city. Finally the lad stops, opens a gate and invites the writer inside. They can hear voices. The yard is deep, with tall papaya trees growing at one end, a banana plantation stifling the other, and, in the middle, a whole profusion of abandoned objects, illuminated by the pale light from the moon. Here the mechanical skeleton of a sewing-machine, a Singer, there an old wooden cot; further on, a large heart in tattered foam. There are a dozen people sitting on plastic chairs, arranged in a semicircle. In the centre, sunk into a mango-yellow sofa, is a very thin, very old woman. A man whose face Uli thinks he recognises brings two more chairs. Uli sits down next to Abdul. The boy translates Dona Cinema's narrative for the writer, in a murmur that flows like a brook. In a fishermen's town, not very far from Muhipiti, men used to have a tradition of gathering at daybreak, whenever there was a full moon, to affix the sky to the firmament and put time into order. The ceremony ensured that the days would follow one another peacefully, with no mistakes or shocks. The fishermen would bring long canes that they would stick into the mud of the mangrove, making different shapes. They did this and they sang.

A girl of six or seven goes from chair to chair, passing out cans of Coke, which are more warm than cold, and meat samosas that are very hot. Uli watches her go, fearful that at any moment the unfortunate child might collapse under the weight of the tray. However, she completes her mission successfully, before disappearing into the house.

"They'd sing," Dona Cinema continues, "and everything would get organised."

Uli pictures the action: slender, very tall men, lifting their incredibly long canes up to infinity, singing and sketching out charms. Then a war happened, and the king who ruled that people died in combat. The fishermen-magicians were scattered around the world. When the full moon came, there was nobody to prop up the sky and to order time. The clouds fell to the ground, helpless. The days went all adrift, tomorrows getting mixed up with yesterdays, people falling asleep today and waking up five days ago, in an extraordinary confusion.

One girl, Mweeri, who was used to watching the ceremony from afar, goes off in search of the long canes. She gathers them up as fast as she can, takes them to the mangrove, and positions them correctly.

"That girl, on her own, she saved the world," concludes Dona Cinema.

Uli returns to the hotel, taking long solitary steps, thinking back to Dona Cinema's stories. He has been left with the feeling that the old lady was making them up as she told them. He is walking beside the sea now. The tide is so high, drawn in by the full moon, that it has consumed the beach.

Then, in a sudden flash, he understands everything.

"She's the girl, she's Mweeri!"

He starts running. He must tell Daniel. A violent pain in his chest, as if somebody has ripped his heart out through his back in a single swipe, stops him in his tracks. He grabs hold of a post, feeling like the night is being emptied of all its light and its oxygen.

"No . . ." he murmurs. "Not like this . . ."

He takes three steps and falls into the sea.

3

Moira and Daniel are lying in bed, with the baby between them. In the diaphanous silence of the night, they can hear one another's hearts. The woman sees the stars hanging from the mosquito net, like Christmas lights, and she is glad because her daughter will grow up on the island, running barefoot along the streets and swimming at the beaches on nights like that one. An "authentic childhood", that's the expression she uses when talking to family and friends, and it's impossible in the big cities, with children shut up in tiny apartments, watching idiotic series on TV, exchanging trivialities on social media or playing on their PlayStation. Her husband thinks about all the good things that life has brought him: love, friends, books, music, sea. He thinks about what life is yet to bring him. The child, this girl, does not think. Her senses, however, absorb and register the intensity of the moment. Fifty years from now, her brain will be hooked up to a computer and she will marvel as she retrieves the distorted images of her parents' faces, the profusion of stars in the immensity of the cosmos, and the sound of three hearts beating, harmoniously out of time.

Ilha de Moçambique, 30 November 2019

Thanks, Notes and a Warning

This novel began to be written out of a short story, "The Builder of Castles", first published in 2012 and which has continued, ever since, to grow inside me. I am hugely grateful to the friends who agreed to read the original manuscript, making corrections and suggesting changes: Catarina Carvalho, Patrícia Reis, Michael Kegler, Lara Longley, Mia Couto and Yara Costa. I would also like to thank my agent, Nicole Witt, for her enthusiasm and her dedication.

Ilha de Moçambique, the Island of Mozambique, also called Muhipiti, has been fascinating poets and writers for centuries. This is due, in part, to the fabulous past of this tiny place, which has been one of the main commercial outposts between Africa and the East. I suspect it is also due to the natural vocation for poetry and for the marvellous that is inherent in most of its inhabitants. Some of the episodes that make up this novel are based on real events. Nevertheless, the characters are the author's own invention, even if, occasionally, they might share a name, or other characteristics, with real people.

My thanks to all of the islanders, who welcomed me like an African brother, opening the doors of their lives to me and agreeing to tell me the stories of the island.

JOSÉ EDUARDO AGUALUSA was born in Huambo in 1960 and is one of the leading literary voices from Angola, and from the Portuguese language today. His first book, *The Conspiracy*, a historical novel set in Sao Paulo de Luanda between 1880 and 1911, paints a fascinating portrait of a society marked by opposites, in which those who can adapt have any chance of success. Creole was awarded the Portuguese Grand Prize for Literature, while *The Book of Chameleons* won the Independent Foreign Fiction Prize in 2007. He and his translator, Daniel Hahn, won the 2017 International Dublin Literary Award for *The General Theory of Oblivion* and the novel was shortlisted for the International Booker Prize. In 2019, Agualusa won Angola's most prestigious literary award, the National Prize for Culture and Arts. Agualusa lives on the Island of Mozambique.

DANIEL HAHN is a writer, editor and translator, with ninety-something books to his name. His translations (from Portuguese, Spanish and French) include fiction, non-fiction, children's books and plays. Recent books include a translation of a Diamela Eltit novel, and *Catching Fire*, his accompanying translation diary.